CU00779917

# THE LONG ARM

Gavin MacDonald

ISBN   978 - 1 - 291 - 76112 - 2

The long arm of coincidence

*Haddon Chambers*

*Detective Chief Inspector Ian Forsyth Books*

Death is my Mistress

The Crime Committee

My Frail Blood

Publish and be Dead

Swallow Them Up

Dishing The Dirt

A Family Affair

Playing Away

Bloody and Invisible Hand

The Truth in Masquerade

I Spy, I Die

A Bow at a Venture

Passport to Perdition

The Plaintive Numbers

The Root of all Evil

Pay Any Price

Murder at he Museum

Murder of an Unknown

The Forsyth Saga

The Second Forsyth Saga

*Science Fiction*

Mysteries of Space and Time

# FOREWORD

For the nineteenth of the novels that I have written about Detective Chief Inspector Ian Forsyth, I have chosen one that occurred fairly early in the period when we worked together as a team. It was given to us to solve in the spring of 1979.

At that time, Forsyth was coming to the peak of his powers and we had been working together for a number of years. I suppose it is difficult for modern-day coppers to believe that Forsyth ever existed and is not a composite of all the inspectors who ever solved a difficult case by logical deduction. Perhaps, in these more strictly regulated times, it would be impossible for someone to flout all the established rules of crime solving, as Forsyth regularly did, and just use his powers of logical reasoning.

As I say, there is doubt among the members of the present-day Force as to whether Forsyth actually existed when they are regaled with tales that seem incredible by grizzled veterans. And, of course, time and the imagination of the storytellers have often added detail to the original stories that is not only hard to believe but is near impossible. And there is no need to add these imaginative extras to the stories for the truth is wonderful enough.

And Forsyth really did exist. I know that only too well. I acted as his sergeant for more years than I care to remember. He was not an easy man to be teamed with, since I was mostly working in the dark because he played his cards so close to his chest. And he left all the routine work, that required no intellectual effort to solve, to his subordinates. We might resent his piling work on us but we all shared in the glory when he solved one of the big ones. And no-one ever asked to be moved from his squad.

I hope that this book helps you to get to know Forsyth better and allows you to wonder at the brilliance of his reasoning.

Alistair MacRae,

Edinburgh, 2014

# CHAPTER 1

The first chapter in the Merton case wasn't even handled by the Forsyth squad, but by the team led by Inspector Hutchison and Sergeant Carter. A man in the process of walking his dog on a fine spring morning on the slopes of Corstorphine Hill, one of the eminences on the west of Edinburgh, couldn't get the animal to come away from a site at which he was scratching. When the owner went to see what it was all about, he observed that what was left of a hand, after being gnawed by animals, was sticking out of the earth. He put in a call to the police after he had got rid of his breakfast, and they dug up what was left of the body of a man in his forties who had been dead for around a month.

It became clear that the dead man was not one of those men on the register of missing persons for the Lothians and Border area, or indeed for any part of Scotland. A reconstruction of the face that had once been attached to the skull was made by a forensic anthropologist and was immediately recognised by the Merton family as a son and brother, Ethan, who had been thought, after the latest in a series of quarrels with the rest of them, to have gone, as he had so often threatened, to seek his fortune in South America.

Each member of the rest of the family was a suspect for the murder because of the innumerable quarrels that Ethan had had with all of them at one time or another. But there were even more likely suspects. The Mertons had for centuries been at loggerheads with a neighbouring family called Douglas and the feud had led over the years to the killing of the odd Merton by a Douglas as well as of the odd Douglas by a Merton. So all Douglases were also in the frame. Ethan had tended to lord it over the inhabitants of the small town of Auchenbland that lay within the confines of the Merton bailliewick, and where the Mertons owned most of the land and property. He had felt that he had the right to dispense justice, or the lack of it, to what he no doubt regarded as the local peasantry, often in a very arbitrary manner. So there were a number of the locals who had grievances against him and could well have murdered him after a night spent acquiring too much to drink in one of the local hostelries. There was therefore no shortage of suspects and a host of people were thoroughly investigated by the Hutchison team over the course of a couple of weeks. But none of the lines of enquiry that the team had pursued had led anywhere and the case had been eventually laid aside to await further developments so that more urgent matters could be attended to by the many officers who had been drafted into the Hutchison team.

It was a month or so after Ethan's body had been unearthed from the sod on Corstorphine Hill that Forsyth's team was sent early one morning to a murder scene at the Merton country house south of Edinburgh. Whether the earlier murder was not remembered when the news of the death at the Merton residence reached the powers that be at Fettes, or whether those who made the decision decided that a fresh approach was necessary, I do not know. All I can say is that I found myself driving the great man out of Edinburgh on one of the roads that led to the south. I hadn't recalled the earlier murder either and so, as I drove, I enquired whether he knew the people whom we were going to see and investigate thoroughly. He is very knowledgeable about the great and good of the area and has met many of them in the course of his private life. And I was not disappointed.

"The Merton son, whose death has caused us to hasten out of Edinburgh, was a solicitor who dealt almost exclusively with conveyancing, but he had a very large practice and was able to make a large amount of money out of it," he said.

"What lawyer doesn't?" I asked.

"It is as you say. But, in the last few years, he has spent less time on his profession and more on looking after the family estate, since his elder brother was not to be trusted to do the job conscientiously. The house to which we are going is the family seat," he went on. "His father and grandfather were wealthy businessmen who made their fortunes, mainly out of engineering of one type or another. You will recall that his elder brother was the man found buried on Corstorphine Hill a short while ago. Whether the two events are related only time will tell."

As I wrote earlier, I had not remembered the event and made the connection. But, now that Forsyth had brought it to my attention, I was able to recall most of the details of the case.

I decided to try to add a little lightness to the proceedings.

"To lose one son may be regarded as a misfortune," I said solemnly. "To lose two looks like carelessness."

"You have obviously been doing some hard work in the literary world," he said with mock admiration, "when you can misquote Oscar Wilde."

I ignored the remark.

"Who is likely to want either or both of the

Mertons dead?" I asked.

"Ethan was a very odd fellow," he told me. "He didn't fit in at all with the country gentleman image that the family would have liked him to cultivate. He refused to pursue any profession and, although the elder son, showed little desire to run the estate and had to be pushed into doing what little interested him. That is why the younger son has been getting involved in keeping the estate functioning smoothly. Ethan continually declared that he needed adventure and got into a number of scrapes here in consequence. So, latterly, he kept proposing to look for the needed adventure overseas, but his parents refused to fund him for these mad enterprises. It was assumed that he had gone off anyway, despite their lack of support, when he disappeared in the wake of the final furious row."

"Didn't they think it odd that he had gone off without informing them?"

"It was par for the course. After a quarrel, he would often not speak to the others for days. And he had often gone off on one of his adventures in the past on the spur of the moment and without letting anyone know where he was going to go."

"So who would have wanted Ethan Merton dead?" I enquired.

"The members of his family for a start. With him out of the way, life for the Mertons could get back to normality. He was the elder son and the estate was entailed and would have to have gone to him. And he felt no need to preserve the family name. If, as was all too likely, he had disposed of all the family assets for cash and moved the proceeds of the sales to Uruguay or wherever he finished up, the Merton presence would have vanished from Scotland and that was something about which his family would not have been happy."

"Are you serious about one of the family killing him to stop the Merton influence dying out?" I asked.

"Perfectly," he replied. "Old families are full of pride and wish their traditions and their influence to continue for all time. And I think that the other son and the daughter would not have relished being done out of their ability to remain in the family seat and continue to lord it over the local peasantry."

"So the parents and a daughter make up the remaining family. Do you see them all as possible murderers?"

"I doubt that the mother or father would kill their elder son. But the other brother, Ralph, whose death we are about to investigate, would have had no hesitation in defending the family honour by getting rid of his brother were that necessary. And the sister, Harriet, is known to be of like mind."

"And now that the second brother has also bitten the dust, the sister will presumably inherit the lot. Quite a motive!"

"The Mertons own a large area round their country estate, including the town of Auchenbland, and exercise almost feudal dominion over the inhabitants of their bailiwick. Their arbitrary decisions, which have altered the fate of some of the locals for the worse, will, I am sure, have made them lots of enemies. Whether any of these so-called common people feel so strongly as to indulge in the murder of their alleged superiors is something we would have to probe."

"So we are going to have no shortage of suspects," I said thoughtfully.

"And, if we add to all that the fact that the Mertons have been at loggerheads for centuries with the family of Douglas, who occupy a position similar to that of the Mertons in an area just to the south of the Merton lands around the town of Darsel, you will find another group of possible suspects. Mertons have been noted in the records to have killed Douglases and Douglases Mertons for a number of centuries. And the feud between the two families has been simmering beneath the surface for some years waiting for a spark to set it alight. Any little thing, apparently trivial to an outside observer, but regarded as a slight by a Douglas, could have resulted in one of that clan deciding to get rid of the odd Merton."

"I didn't realise that Scotland still contained such warring tribes."

"You only have to go to any Celtic–Rangers match," Forsyth pointed out, "and you will see two tribes, separated by different religious beliefs, behaving like primitive savages."

"You do have a point. But I had not thought that this tribalism extended to the landed gentry."

"Anything that the poor get up to," said the Inspector, "the gentry do, admittedly with more subtlety, but with even more ferocity."

We sat in silence for the rest of the journey, both thinking of the problems that lay ahead.

The Merton estate was vast. We turned off the A7 and drove along a minor road before we got to it. Our approach to the estate was through stone pillars, each of which had on its flat top a mythical creature, neither of which I was able to identify. The gates that the pillars held were standing open and seemed to be in good repair. We drove for what must have been over half a  mile before we came  to the big house.  The grounds through which we drove were in excellent nick and included what appeared to be a nine-hole golf course, tennis courts and a bowling green, indicating that the Merton family was not short of the necessary readies.

The house itself looked like a set from a film of Brideshead Revisited,  It looked to my unpractised eye like a mish-mash of styles stuck together to form rather a pleasing whole.  It was three storeys high with an attic layer above and had assorted turrets at the corners of the roof.  I had little time to see more as Forsyth hurried towards the front door and I was forced to follow.  We made our way through a number of cars parked in the area in front of the house and entered through a portico into a large well-appointed hall where DC Andy Beaumont awaited us to brief the Chief on the latest killing.

"Morning, sir," he said. "The dead man is Ralph Merton who lived here with his father, mother and sister. The killer seems to have broken in to the house via a French window on the ground floor in the middle of the night, crept up to Ralph's bedroom and hit him on the head with the usual blunt instrument while he was asleep before torturing and then suffocating him. The rest of the household, which includes three live-in servants, claim to have heard not a thing."

"Right!" said Forsyth. "We had better start by having a look at the body."

Andy took us to a magnificent staircase that led to the upper regions. We mounted on a thick and expensive stair carpet to the first floor and made our way to a bedroom at the back of the house. It was lavishly furnished, the bed being a four-poster and the rest of the furniture being similarly old-fashioned and made from solid oak. The carpet had a thick pile and the curtains were of a rich and expensive material.

The bedclothes had been pushed from the bed and were lying on the floor along with the pillow that had been used to suffocate the dead man and a pair of pyjamas. On the bed was the naked body of Ralph

Merton. He had a strip of masking tape pressed down over his mouth, his face holding a look of fear and horror. His arms were tied behind his back and his legs were twisted in odd positions. There were marks on his body where burning cigarettes had been placed and blood had oozed from where cuts had been made on his torso and limbs. Leaning over the body of Merton was Dr Hay, the police surgeon, while a man from forensics was practising his trade near the dressing table.

Dr Hay saw us entering and left his position by the bed to join us, taking a cigar case from his pocket as he did so, removing from it an evil-smelling cheroot, lighting it and puffing happily on it before he spoke. The police surgeon was in his late forties, a rotund figure who peered benevolently at the world through thick pebble spectacles. He was wearing the usual shapeless clothes and had, on his head, the battered old soft hat without which he was never seen. Rumour had it that he slept in these garments as well. He was reputed to have no interest in life other than medicine and the only thing that was alleged to stir his heart was the thrill of expectation at the moment when he had a knife poised to slice into the latest victim on his mortuary table. But he was one of the best quacks in the business and you could rely one hundred per cent on what he told you about a victim.

"Not a lot to help you here," he told us. "The poor bugger was hit over the head, while still asleep, with the usual blunt instrument to keep him silent, had his hands tied behind his back and his mouth sealed up so that he couldn't scream and he was then tortured before being suffocated with a pillow. That's a good way to kill someone. No mess and no tell-tale traces to get you caught. Crooks are learning too much of how to keep out of trouble these days. It's all these silly cop shows that abound on television. They should all be banned."

"Was Merton being tortured to reveal some secret he held or was the killer merely having sadistic fun with the victim?" I asked.

"Since the tape was never removed from the mouth, I doubt that the killer wanted any information. He seems to have been taking revenge for some real or imagined hurt from the past."

"Time of death?" I enquired.

"Round about two this morning, give or take a couple of hours either way. I'll be more precise after the *post mortem.* The one thing that might be of interest to you is the knot on the rope that is around Merton's wrists. I've seen a few knots in my time but this is something I haven't come across before."

He turned Merton over so that we could get a good look at the knot on the rope that bound the wrists. To me, one knot looks like another but Forsyth was clearly interested.

"It looks somewhat like the knots that fishermen on the West Coast used to use but it seems to have an extra loop on it," he observed. "We had better take a close-up picture of it and see if we can get anyone to tell us who uses such knots."

"I have already taken some polaroids of the

knot," said the forensic man, having heard what Forsyth had said.

"Excellent," said the Chief.

"Well, that's my lot," said Hay. "So, if there are no more questions, I'll be on my way. I have a busy schedule this morning."

And with that he gathered up his bag and left, a tuneless whistle and a whiff of cheap cigar smoke drifting after him.

The man from forensics, whom I hadn't come across before, grudgingly admitted that he had so far found nothing of interest. I asked him, since he had obviously had a look at the rope with which Merton had been tied, if there was a possibility that we could find out where the rope had been bought.

"Not a chance," he said. "That kind of rope is sold in practically all hardware and DIY stores. In addition, that piece of rope is by no means new. It has been used for something before this. So it may have been bought years ago."

I sighed. Another possible lead had just gone

up in smoke. After a tour of the room, in which he seemed to find nothing of interest, Forsyth indicated that he would like to have a look at the window through which the intruder had made his entry. Beaumont took us to the French window in the sitting room on the ground floor.

The door of the French windows had ten panes of glass in it, two at each horizontal level. The two at the level of the door handle had both been cut out with a glass cutter and had been leaned up against the outside wall of the house. A key was sticking in the outside of the lock on the door.

"Where did the key that is in the lock come from?" asked the Chief.

"The key was kept on that hook in the wall that you can see about six feet away from the door on the right as we look at the door now," Andy replied. "Once the intruder had taken the two panes out of the window, he was able to reach in with a pole or a wire with a hook on the end and fish out the key."

"But why take two panes out," asked Forsyth

thoughtfully, "when to take out one would have done just as well?"

"Maybe he found it easier that way," Beaumont suggested.

"It might be so. And, of course," Forsyth added, "we must not lose sight of the fact that anyone from inside the house who wanted to kill Ralph and make it look as if the crime had been committed by an outsider, could easily remove the panes of glass from the French window after opening the door from the inside and stepping out onto the lawn."

"So you think that it was Ralph's sister who did it?" I said

"It is too early to be able to attach blame. I merely point out that the fact that panes have been removed from the French window does not mean that the killer necessarily came from outside."

We decided to use the library as a convenient room in which to conduct interviews and Beaumont left us to it. Mrs Merton, not surprisingly after her earlier loss, appeared to have been very much affected by the death of her second son and her husband was not keen for her to be interviewed on her own.  So we had both parents brought in to the library together.

Gilbert Merton was in his late fifties.  He had been at one time in the Army and was still as straight as a ramrod. He had a thin face with high cheek bones and a large nose. His brown hair was liberally sprinkled with white, which he made no effort to disguise.  He was wearing a white shirt, open at the neck, expensive slacks with knife-like creases showing, a cashmere sweater and brown brogues. He sat down in an upright chair in front of us after helping his wife into a chair alongside, folded his hands in his lap and waited for our questions.

Angela Merton was tall but the tragedy of the loss of her sons seemed to be weighing her down and she appeared to be bent over.  She had dressed hurriedly and had not put on make-up so that she appeared as if recovering from an illness.  She sat listlessly in her chair and seemed hardly aware of our presence.

"At what time was the body of your son found and by whom?" asked Forsyth.

"Our daughter," said the father, "went into his room to rouse him, since they had arranged to go together to a lecture in Edinburgh this morning. This was at around 7 o'clock."

"And no-one in the household had heard anything during the night?"

"Not as far as we know."

"Have you any idea as to who would wish your son harm?" I asked.

That simple remark roused Mrs Merton from her torpor.

"Do you need to ask?" she shouted in a loud voice. "It's the same people who killed Ethan. The people who have wanted us all dead for centuries. That horrible Douglas clan have always been intent on killing us all off. They covet our lands. They envy us. They would do anything to get rid of us and take over."

Merton put his arm round her to soothe her and stroked her forehead.

"Don't get yourself all upset," he said.

Then he turned to us.

"But what she says is true. Look to the Douglas clan for your killer."

We got nothing further of interest from them and had the daughter brought in for interview. She turned out to be on the tall side with a plain face decorated by the large nose which seemed to be a characteristic of the Mertons and dark hair that hung rather limply round her head. She was dressed in shapeless clothes that did nothing to enhance her appearance. It struck me that someone as unattractive as she was might well believe that she needed to ensure her future by making sure that she, and not her brothers, inherited a great deal of money.

"It was you who found your brother's body," suggested Forsyth.

"It was," she replied soberly. "We had intended to go to a lecture together this morning and I went to waken him when he didn't appear to be up."

"Have you any idea as to who would have wished him dead?" enquired the Chief.

"I am sure that you have been told that the Douglases have always hated the Mertons. And have killed a few of us in their time. And that the murder of Ralph is merely another in the long line of crimes committed by the Douglass against the Mertons."

"And, of course, the Mertons have also disposed of a few of the Douglas clan in times gone by," the Chief pointed out.

"That, of course, is very true," she admitted with a slight smile appearing on her face. "But it does not automatically mean that the Douglases are responsible for Ralph's death."

"It would appear from your tone," suggested Forsyth, "that you do not believe that the Douglas clan is as bad as they have been painted."

"We are no longer living in the Middle Ages. We should not be at daggers drawn with one another all the time."

"But your parents would not appear to share your views."

"Nor did my brothers. But I can see no reason why a Douglas, if he wished to kill a Merton, should do so by sneaking into our house to kill Ralph in the middle of the night."

"So you think that we should be looking elsewhere for the murderer," I came in. "If I do look in other directions, I note that you will now inherit the Merton estate when your father dies. Some might think that that gives you a very strong motive for getting rid of your brother."

She stared at me with a frown on her brow for a moment or two.

"Some might," she agreed. "But fratricide is not one of my defects."

"How many people would know that the key needed to open the French window was kept hanging close by?" I asked.

"Anyone who has ever been to the house would be aware of it."

"And how many of the local people would that include?"

"We hold a party once a year for those of the population of the area who run our local services, the Town Council, shops and the like.  That includes quite a lot of the townspeople."

"What about the Douglases?"

"It is necessary for all of us to work together these days. The Douglases have been in this house in the sitting room at meetings of the local Conservative party or conferences about local interests.  Though we do not get on with them, we have to put up with them in the course of everyday life.  The open hostility that once existed has had to give way to a more civilised attitude in these more enlightened times."

"Can you think of anyone, other than one of the Douglas clan,  who would wish to have your brother dead?" I enquired.

"He has been involved," she replied, "in looking after our properties in Auchenbland. The decisions that he has made often affect the lives of some of the inhabitants detrimentally, and he can sometimes be a trifle arbitrary in his decision making. And people are often unable to see the logic of decisions when they themselves are involved. If some of those affected resent what has been decided for them, they could well feel resentment against Ralph. But whether that would make them resort to torturing and murdering him is another matter."

"And you heard nothing at all of what was going on during the night?"

"I am a very heavy sleeper."

We allowed her to leave and then interviewed the servants individually but they all slept on the attic floor and all claimed to have heard nothing untoward during the night. It was possible that one of them might have killed Ralph for whatever reason but, until we came across a motive for one of them to do so, we removed them from the list of suspects.

"Do you think," I asked as we went out to the car, "that we have a Montague and Capulet situation here? The attitude of Harriet to the feud is so different from that of her parents that I wonder if she has a romantic attachment to one of the Douglases."

"Well!" he said. "We are very literary today. First you quote from *The Importance of Being Earnest* and now you are reprising the plot of *Romeo and Juliet.* Do you see everything through the medium of plays?"

I ignored his sally and he gave some thought to the matter before he carried on.

"I suppose your notion about Miss Merton is possible. We will need to enquire as to whether Miss Merton has a romantic attachment."

"Where to now?" I asked.

"I think it would be sensible to pay a visit to the Douglas household, since they are certainly no friends of the Mertons, to see what each of them claims to have been doing during last night."

# CHAPTER 2

It was quite a short drive to the Douglas country seat, since the lands that the Mertons and Douglases owned were almost adjacent to one another. It turned out to be a house that had become larger over the years as successive generations of Douglases had added more and more additions to the main building, not all of which blended in well with the original architect's vision. The house was reached by a long driveway from the main road and I noted that the Douglases, like the Mertons, seemed to be not short of a bob or two, since the grounds were in immaculate order.

When I plied the massive knocker on the front door, we could hear the sound it produced echoing through the hallway and the noise eventually summoned a servant who regarded us with some suspicion and then reluctantly allowed us to enter when we showed our warrant cards. We were conducted to a well-furnished sitting room where we had to wait several minutes before Sir Geoffrey

Douglas appeared. He was a stocky man, on the short side, with a round, red face and prominent ears. He had a shock of thick, reddish hair on his round head and was dressed in tweeds over a white shirt and regimental tie. His shoes were so highly polished that I am sure he was able to see his face in them.

"You're not from the local police station," he observed when he saw us.

"No. We are from Edinburgh," I informed him. "This is Detective Chief Inspector Forsyth and I am Detective Sergeant MacRae. We are investigating the murder of Ralph Merton which took place last night."

"So young Merton is dead. Not that his passing will cause any grief in this house. You will be well aware that our two households have been enemies for the best part of three centuries."

"Which is why we would like to know in what way all the members of this household spent their time during last night."

"So you think that one of us was responsible for killing him?"

"We would like to be able to eliminate you all from our enquiries," I said tactfully.

"Very well," he said. "My wife, as you may know, is bedridden. I sat with her for a while after dinner and we watched a television programme together. Then I went to the office that I have here and dealt with a number of matters concerning the estate. Then I had a whisky to drink while I was reading a book before I took myself to bed at around ten thirty. My wife and I sleep in separate rooms because of her condition. I was there until seven o'clock this morning."

"Can anyone confirm all this?" I asked.

"I did not have some wench from the village coming to my bed, if that is what you are implying. That is not my style. So no."

"But your sons or the servants might be able to say that you never left the house."

"The servants had the night off as there was a

dance taking place in the village. My two sons were out for the evening, goodness knows where. They are adults. I do not insist on knowing where it is that they are spending the evening."

"Then that is all that we need from you at the moment. But we would like to speak to your sons, if it is convenient," said Forsyth.

"I will send them to you," Douglas said and left.

It took some time for Basil Douglas to join us and I assumed that he had had to be pulled from his bed. This supposition was confirmed when he entered the room, looking sleepy, with tousled hair, and clad in a dressing gown over rather flashy pyjamas. He was taller than his father and with a good deal of beef on his frame. He had the same red hair and large ears. He had a large glass of what looked like orange juice in his hand and he took draughts from this at intervals during the interview.

"I gather," he said, "that Ralph Merton has kicked the bucket and you want to find out whether I had a hand in his demise."

"Had you?" Forsyth asked.

"Definitely not. The Douglas clan stopped slitting the throats of Mertons over fifty years ago. We try to appear to be civilised these days."

"So how were you occupying yourself last night?" I enquired.

"There was a dance in the nearest village. I attended it. And, being the handsome, eldest son of the squire of these parts, I find that I am popular with the ladies. One of them was kind enough to invite me to spend the night with her. It would have been churlish of me not to have accepted."

"And the lady's name?"

"I will not give you that unless I am charged with the murder of Ralph, in which I had no part. One has to play the chivalrous lover and prevent a lady's name from being sullied, has one not?"

"Enquiries that we make among other people who attended the function may reveal the name of the lady with whom you left the dance," I pointed out. "Why not save us a good deal of time and energy?"

"I cannot prevent you from trying to find out the lady's name but I will not help you to do so."

"Have you any suggestions as to who, apart from members of the Douglas clan, might have wished Merton dead?"

"He, like all the Mertons," said Basil, "treated the inhabitants of Auchinbland and the surrounding area like vassals who should have no say in their own destiny. As a result, a number have suffered grievously at the hands of those who are alleged to be their superiors and many a deep resentment lies just below the surface. One of those wronged may have found the courage to do something about it.

"It may also have reached your ears that the Mertons are proposing to give a mining company the right to work a quarry on their land. A few houses will have to be knocked down to make way for the access road, and a number of those living nearby will be subject to a considerable amount of noise and a good deal of air pollution. A committee has been formed to try to stop the proposed development, led by a man called Ewan Grant, who is one of those who will be most affected by the new scheme. Since planning permission has just been granted for the quarry, it is not impossible that Grant, or one of the other members of the committee has decided that more drastic measures are required."

Callum Douglas followed his elder brother. He looked very like him, with red, unruly hair and big ears but he was smaller and there was a mean cast to his face. He was dressed casually in a tee shirt and jeans which he had obviously slipped on hurriedly when he had been pulled from his bed. He came into the room, sat down and eyed us suspiciously.

"You will have heard that Ralph Merton has been murdered," said the Chief.

"And why should you believe that we had anything to do with it?" he answered angrily. "The days when the Douglases went around sticking swords into Mertons are long gone."

"So where were you last night?"

"I went to the dance that was taking place locally but I found that it was a bit of a bore, so I went for a drive. I had a notion to see the ocean, so I went to the coast. I fell asleep while I was there and didn't get back here until about three am."

"And presumably no-one saw you while you were there?"

"I certainly didn't see anyone."

"So, no alibi," I pointed out

"I don't need one," he insisted "I haven't done anything."

I decided to try to see if one of my notions had any substance.

"I understand that both you and Harriet Merton believe that the feud between your two families is quite absurd and out of date and that it should be stopped as quickly as possible."

There was a moment's hesitation before Douglas replied. Then he reluctantly agreed that that was so.

"In fact you were not at the ocean at all, you

were discussing, with Harriet, among other things, how to get the feud stopped."

He had gone a trifle pale and there was a longer interval before he spoke.

"I hope you are not going to make such a suggestion to my parents," he said at length.

"Whatever information is revealed to us in interviews here today," I informed him, "will be kept confidential at all times unless it is necessary to use it in court during the trial of whoever killed Ralph Merton. Your secret is safe with us."

"In that case," he said, "I will admit that you are correct. Harriet and I are very much attracted to one another. We have, naturally, kept this fact from our parents, both sets of whom would go ballistic at the thought that we were not all the time at each other's throats. And you will understand that we want the feud stopped as soon as possible."

"So you two were together from some time like 11pm last night until 3am this morning," suggested Forsyth.

"We were."

"Exactly where?"

"There is an unoccupied cottage near the boundary of this estate. It is easily reached from a little-used minor road so that there is little likelihood of us being seen getting to it. And our cars can be kept well out of sight from the road."

"And you have no idea who would wish to torture and kill Ralph?"

"Certainly not my brother nor I. One of the people from Auchenbland perhaps who has been given a raw deal. And there are quite a few of these."

As we walked from the house, Forsyth smiled warmly at me.

"So your notion that the young lovers were doing a Romeo and Juliet act was correct. And you managed to find the correct way of getting him to admit that it was true. Very well done."

I always feel chuffed when Forsyth praises something I have done, so I had a bit of a warm glow wrapping me.

"What he doesn't seem to realise," I pointed out, "is that the two of them must now be right in the frame for the murder. They have only each other as alibis and the best way to kill off the feud once and for all is for Harriet to become boss of the Merton outfit and possibly Callum to become the same in the Douglas household. So maybe the death of Basil is to come or perhaps Basil is of the same mind as Callum that the feud has gone on long enough and it won't be necessary to eliminate him too."

"The pair are certainly high on the list of suspects," Forsyth said sagely.

"Do you want to go to Auchinbland," I asked, "to see if any of the inhabitants of the place on which Ralph Merton has done the dirty in the past are likely to have exacted their revenge?"

"I will leave that to the team. That is the part of the investigation at which you are expert. In addition, I think that you should be trying to find out whether anyone, particularly Miss Merton or a

Douglas, was seen around during the night."

"I will see to that. Did anything strike you about the murder?"

"I think that the knot is of interest and might lead somewhere.  And I still find it odd that the intruder should have found it necessary to take out two panes of glass from the French window."

# CHAPTER 3

We got back to Police Headquarters at Fettes in Edinburgh just after lunch time. Forsyth disappeared to his office, no doubt to let that massive brain of his ponder on the events of the morning. But, although I was quite keen to get something to eat, I thought it right to go off in search of Bill Carter.

Detective Sergeant Carter was one of the few sergeants, when I was a struggling PC on the beat, who was prepared to give helpful advice to someone striving to learn the business and I had found him just as helpful when I was a struggling newly promoted detective sergeant trying to learn how to cope with a superior like Forsyth. Bill had given the team valuable information in the case involving the murder of an Edinburgh wine and spirits merchant called Lamont which I chronicled under the title *Death is my Mistress.* He had grown old in the police service without ever making it to Inspector. His face was round and bore evidence of too many drinks consumed on and off duty during the long years spent as a detective. The hair surmounting it was grizzled. His body had too much stomach, again from the drinks and also from the fast food consumed in a hurry on duty or surveillance, but was otherwise in good shape.

I found Bill hunched over his desk writing a report and, greeting him warmly, offered him a cigarette. He accepted, looked up at me as we lit up and a grin appeared on his face.

"I heard your lot got stuck with the latest Merton murder," he said. "Since we got nowhere with the previous one, the powers-that-be in their wisdom gave this one to Forsyth. And, since you have found no clues at the country seat, you have come to pick my brains to see if I can help."

"I thought," I replied, "that if I bought you a drink, the alcohol might lubricate your brain cells sufficiently for you to reveal all the things that your team found out about Ethan Merton's death but kept from the public and press. Then our combined well-oiled brainpower might spot something that might lead to a solution of both crimes that will dazzle and astound the Chief Super."

"I see that you are still the romantic optimist even after being in this job for more years than you care to remember. But I am always happy for you to put your hand in your pocket and buy me a drink."

So we repaired to the waterhole that a lot of us often frequented when the day's work was done. It lies roughly half way between Fettes and the Crematorium and is comfortable without being too fancy and doesn't attract either the financial wizards or the criminal element. I purchased two pints of heavy and two whiskies at the bar counter and we took these to a table away from the crowd around the bar.

I gave Bill a quick resume of all we had seen and heard that morning. He sat quietly absorbing it all and, when I had finished, thought for a few minutes before saying anything.

"Not much there that you can really get your

teeth into," he ventured at length. "The Romeo and Juliet pair might well have done it, though it might be a right bugger to prove. And the torture doesn't seem likely from them, though I suppose that that may be a conclusion that we are supposed to come to and rule them out."

"Were there any similar features with Ethan Merton's killing?" I asked.

"The body had been in the ground for a few weeks before it was discovered, so things weren't as straightforward as if we had got to the corpse at once. There was no evidence that the wrists had been tied together before death, nor was there any rope in the grave with the body. But it was pretty certain that Ethan had been subjected to some kind of torture. Both legs had been broken and his body had subjected to a number of cuts. These, of course, were facts that we kept to ourselves."

"So it looks as if the same killer was responsible for both murders."

"Unless the second is a copy-cat killing."

"But, since you never released the fact that the body had been tied up and tortured," I pointed out, "it would have to be a member of your team or someone close to it who did the copying and that seems a little unlikely."

Bill had to agree and we mulled the thing over while we finished the drinks and had a refill. But I had no more notions about the crime at the end of our discussion than I had had at the beginning.

We returned to the nick and I gathered the team around me before I went for something to eat in the canteen. It was time to distribute tasks among them. Andy Beaumont was given the tasks of trying to find out as much as he could about Harriet Manson and the two Douglas sons, including whether any of them had been seen out and about the previous night. This was a task right up Andy's street.

Andy's a little on the short side for a policeman but he has two qualities that make him invaluable to the Force. The first is that he can pass for an average Joe anywhere. Once he's left you, you find it difficult to think of any characteristic with which to describe him. He can melt into a crowd and find out what's going on without anyone giving him a second glance. His build is average and he has an ordinary, unmemorable, innocent face, mousy brown hair and clothes indistinguishable from his neighbour's.

His second great virtue is that he could worm information from a tailor's dummy. When you talk to him, you get the impression that he's drinking in every word and that what you are saying is the most important thing in the world. He's the perfect listener and that, allied to his ready sympathy and ordinary appearance, means that neighbours, tradesmen and servants open their heart to him when any other copper would find them silent and resentful. Beaumont would be able to pick up all the gossip about the Mertons and Douglases that was in circulation and, at the same time, would be keeping his ears open for anything noteworthy that was being said about other possible suspects.

To Sid Fetcher and myself, I assigned the tasks of going around different parts of Auchenbland and the surrounding area getting lists of all the people who had been done down by one or other of the Merton sons and who were likely to have sufficient motive for torturing and killing the pair in consequence. In particular, I was going to concentrate on finding out all that I could about the quarry project and the feelings of the protestors towards the people who had secretly planned it so that it could go ahead before anyone knew anything about it. Would they have believed that the killing of the Merton sons would put an end to the whole idea?

Sid is a tall, lean, cadaverous individual, forty years old and with a gloomy expression and thinning, black hair. He's been the longest of all of us on Forsyth's team and will remain there till retirement. His many years in the force have convinced him that it will always be his fate to be the one left holding the short straw, and his wife leaving him, unable to stand the amount of time she was left on her own and the cold-shouldering by some of the neighbours, did nothing to lessen that view. But he carries on his work with great determination to show that he will not let the fates get him down. And he is fiercely loyal to Forsyth who is the one rock to which he can cling in the shifting sands of life. But he is also not the brightest of individuals.

To Martin Jenkins I gave the task of going through the local archives to see whether either or both of the sons had been involved in any incident that might lead a victim of the incident to seek revenge. I felt that our most recent recruit might be more suited to such an academic exercise than to having close encounters with members of the local populace.

Martin had been with the team for only a few months but had been blooded in a couple of major murder investigations. He is the very epitome of clean-limbed youth. He's tall and spare, snappily dressed, with a keen, eager face and wavy hair trimmed to regulation length. He would make a good model for a more youthful, more innocent Sherlock Holmes from the time before he met the good Dr Watson. A recent recruit, armed with a degree and convinced that a Chief Constable's baton is already nestling in his knapsack and will be brought into use in record time, he gives all the appearance of a trained bloodhound tugging impatiently at the leash. Most of his superiors tend to treat his enthusiasm indulgently, while missing no opportunity to rub his nose in the messier parts of the routine of police work. But he brings out the worst in Forsyth who, no doubt, recognises in the young man certain of his own less endearing qualities.

CHAPTER 4

When I got back from an afternoon spent in digging for dirt in Auchenbland, I went to the office that I share with three others in the Police Headquarters and wrote up all that I had learned. Only then did I make for the pub in which I had drunk with Bill Carter earlier in the day. I found that the three other members of the team were already there, ensconced at a table far enough from the bar and other tables so that none of the words of wisdom that we came up with would find their way into any flapping ears that might be around and appear in garbled form in the *Scotsman* the next morning. Beaumont and Fletcher sat as usual with pints of heavy in front of them, while Jenkins, who was not a beer drinker, indeed not a great drinker of any alcoholic beverage, was toying with a gin and tonic. I purchased a pint of heavy at the bar and went over and joined them at their table.

Any team of Forsyth's that I run will always meet in the pub of an evening during a major investigation in order to discuss the case. And there is a good reason why we do it in the pub and not in the nick in the company of the great man. Forsyth always plays his cards close to his chest. He suffered an acrimonious divorce from his former wife where lots of things that he had said came back in a form that told against him and, probably because of that unedifying experience, he does not ever wish it to be known that he has said or done anything that might be considered to be wrong. And, having gone down that route, he has now got himself into a position where he wants to be regarded as infallible at all times. So he keeps his thoughts to himself until he is absolutely sure that he has got everything right. In consequence, we mere mortals work in the dark until he has solved the case and is prepared to dazzle us with the brilliance of his reasoning.

Most of those who work for Forsyth accept this philosophically, since his method of working has brought spectacular results. But one rather bolshy Detective Constable  once complained to him that he was unhappy at being treated like a cypher and kept totally in the dark. Forsyth's reply was simple. He pointed out that his method worked very successfully. So, only if one of his team arrived at the solution of a mystery before, or even at the same time as, he did would he think of changing his *modus operandi*. He also added that, should such an unlikely event occur, he would proclaim the triumph of his minion from the rooftops and would also present the successful solver with a crate of the finest malt whisky.

Since that time, all teams have attempted to arrive at the solution of a major case before Forsyth does. This is not because we wish him to change his method of working which has been spectacularly successful, though a little more enlightenment during a case would be very welcome. But we are intent on winning that crate of whisky to show him that, at least on one occasion, we can beat him to the punch. I have to admit that so far we have not been able to achieve our ambition.

After I had sat down and taken a refreshing swallow of beer, I asked Andy Beaumont if he would give the first report. He had a quick draught from his pint before he spoke, in order to make sure that his tubes were sufficiently lubricated.

"Both the Merton sons had a bad reputation in Auchenbland. For the last five years, the old man has sat back and enjoyed a quiet life and left the sons to look after all the affairs of the estate. And, because Ethan, although the elder son, was such a pillock, both sons were given joint responsibility for running everything. But, unlike their father before them, who was regarded as pretty fair on the whole, they made all sorts of arbitrary decisions, some of which had a major impact on people's lives. For example, about a year ago they had a major look at how efficiently the properties that they owned in Auchenbland were being run and whether the estate was getting what they regarded as sufficient return from their investment. A number of people were turfed out of homes or businesses that some of them had rented for years. And the general opinion was that a lot of the decisions were flawed and that a number of families had been put on the breadline quite wrongly."

He stopped and had another go at his pint.

"And who," I asked, "were those whose families were suddenly at the poor house door and who might feel that revenge should be exacted?"

"Colin MacCallum, who for years had run the main hotel in the town, The Merton Arms, and some thought with reasonable success, was suddenly thrown out and replaced without warning. The same happened to Bill Mathers, who ran the grocer's shop and Tony Fisher who had the local boutique. At the same time, Angus MacTavish and Willie Campbell were, without warning, thrown out of the houses they had lived in for many years. One might argue that, since the latter two had been the subject of complaints from time to time by their neighbours, they perhaps deserved what they got. But it was generally felt that the other three had been hard done by and that in all cases a little more mercy should have been shown. Willie Campbell is a bit too old to be going around murdering people. But the general feeling is that, if one of the others is responsible for the two deaths, good luck to them. The Mertons have only got what they deserved."

"Interesting," I said. "Tomorrow, we had better look into the movements of these new suspects at the times of the murders. Any joy on the sightings of the Douglas sons and Harriet Merton?"

"No-one that I spoke to had any notion that Harriet Merton and a Douglas were linked in any way. So they have managed to be very discreet. And I could find no-one who had glimpsed Harriet or a Douglas out and about around the time of Ralph's killing. But you may find it interesting that, after a few enquiries, I found out the name of the girl with whom Basil left the dance and I had a talk with her. She is adamant that Basil did not spend the night at her place. But whether he has been lying to us or she is concealing the truth to preserve her reputation, her parents being very strict, I would not like to guess. I think each is equally likely. I haven't spoken to him, but she struck me as liable to insist on whatever was in her best interest as she saw it."

Andy returned to his beer and I invited Malcolm Jenkins to tell us how he had got on. He obviously enjoyed his moment of being in the limelight.

"Ethan Merton," he told us, "had a bit of a temper and he didn't take kindly to any of the peasants being uppity and talking back to him. And he was quite an athletic sort of person. So he had been up in the local court on a couple of occasions for assault, after two of the locals felt aggrieved at his treatment of them and reported him. One of the assaults was quite serious with the victim ending up in hospital. But, of course, the baillies who tried the cases were cronies of the Mertons and Ethan was handed out a light community sentence in one case and a suspended sentence in the other."

"Who were the pair who were assaulted and

then did not get justice?" I quizzed.

"Andy has mentioned both of the victims already," Jenkins replied. "They were Colin MacCallum and Bill Mathers."

"Who had already been done out of their livelihoods by Ethan and Ralph and so tried to have it out with Ethan and got beaten up for their pains. I think you had better, along with Andy, do an in-depth survey into the lives of these two since they got thrown out of their jobs and into what their movements were last night."

"I will be happy to do that," said Jenkins. "I also found out that both Ethan and Ralph were witnesses about twelve months ago to a motor accident caused by a fellow called Martin Goff who knocked over and killed a child on the edge of Auchenbland when out driving and then didn't stop."

"Did he get sent to prison and is he out now?" asked Fletcher.

"Goff denied strenuously," said Jenkins, ignoring the question, "that he had hit and killed anyone in his car, although there was a dent on the wing that could have been caused by the car hitting something. He claimed that the damage had happened much earlier, but there was no independent confirmation and he was found guilty on the evidence of the Mertons."

"If, as I assume, or you wouldn't be bringing the matter up, he is out now," I pointed out, "that means that he only got a sentence of two years and has got out, after serving half, for good behaviour. It's the minimum sentence you can get for that type of offence and it seems to me to be a mite lenient for causing the death of a child and then not stopping after the accident."

"As I say," explained Jenkins, "Goff denied hitting the child, but he had been drinking and may well have been over the limit at the time of the accident although, when the police eventually found him, he was under the limit. The Mertons told the court that it was at least possible that he hadn't known about the accident because the kid was in the shadow of a building and was wearing dark clothing. Goff's car went over a pot-hole at the time he hit the child and the bump caused by the car hitting the body would not have been noticed."

"So, although he might resent the fact that the Mertons had clyped to the police," said Beaumont, "they also saved him from a much longer prison sentence. Is there enough there to make him turn into a vindictive murderer?"

"People have funny notions as to what demands revenge and what doesn't," I said judiciously. "We keep him in as a suspect and we will see if we can find out what his views on the Mertons are and what he was doing during the wee hours of last night."

Sid Fletcher informed us that he had gone round a good part of Auchenbland and its surroundings and had talked to as many people as were prepared to open their hearts to him about the Mertons.

"And that wasn't all that many," he admitted. "I

don't have Andy's ability to worm my way into their confidence and I think that a lot of them were afraid that any criticism that they made of the Mertons would get back to the big house and that they would suffer the same fate as MacCallum or Mathers."

"Understandable," suggested Beaumont.

"But it was the general feeling of those who were prepared to open up to me that Ethan had been an odd ball who didn't really fit in or know what he really wanted to do and that, in consequence, he had a short temper and was prepared to take out his frustration on other people. Ralph was more rational and more approachable but was very conscious of the fact that he was a Merton and that the rest of them were plebs. He was quite likely to make arbitrary decisions without regard to the effect that they might have on other people's lives. The throwing out of people from their livelihoods or houses a year ago was widely quoted and it was felt strongly that those who had suffered most from the decisions made at that time were perfectly capable of knocking off the Mertons who had caused all their distress. And the general consensus seemed to be that the young Mertons were only getting their just deserts."

"But why wait a year to take their revenge?" asked Jenkins. "Why not kill them at the time that the distress was caused?"

"People are optimists," suggested Beaumont. "The killer possibly thought that it would turn out all right in the end. He would expect to get another job or home as good as the one he had lost and get back to a reasonable standard of living. It would only be when all hopes were dashed that his mind would turn to getting revenge for the sufferings that the Mertons had caused him and his family to go through."

"That's a fair point," I said. "So which of the five thrown out during the clear-out got back to a decent kind of life and which didn't?"

"Fisher and his family upped stakes and moved with their stock to Darsel. He opened a similar boutique there and has done well. But MacCallum had to take a menial job to survive and he and his family now have a standard of living much worse than they could have expected a couple of years ago. MacCallum had always assumed that his son would, in the course of time, take over the running of the hotel from him. Since he is not a very bright kid, his future now seems very much up in the air."

Since he had begun to sound a little hoarse, Fletcher had a couple of swallows of beer to soothe his throat before continuing.

"Mathers hasn't worked since he was evicted from the grocer's shop and is living on benefits. His family lives on an estate where the kids tend to roam around in gangs and cause all sorts of damage. His children have had to move to the estate school where the education supplied is not of the highest order and where they have to mix with some hard cases. One of the boys is already causing concern by wanting to become a gang member."

"It's when it starts to hurt your kids that you become very belligerent to people who have done you down," Beaumont observed.

"Both MacTavish and Campbell, who got evicted from their houses are managing in accommodation which is very much worse that they enjoyed before," Fletcher went on. "And both resent what has happened to them and their families. Goff had a period, while he was in prison, when his family were homeless, where his wife had a bit of a breakdown, so that the family was therefore split up, the children being placed with foster families and moved around a lot, so that they could never settle anywhere. He believes, and it is almost certainly correct, that his wife's present poor health and the children's discipline problems are a direct result of that period in their lives."

"So, leaving Campbell out of it," I suggested, "because of his age and frailty, we still have three, possibly four, suspects with excellent motives, who may have been nursing their wrath to keep it warm as they struggled to better themselves and eventually realised that that wasn't going to happen and all they had left was the possibility of revenge."

"Did you find out anything more in your probings?" Beaumont asked me.

"My experience was the same as Sid's," I admitted. "A lot of people were afraid that I would report anything they said to the Mertons. Most agencies around here, including the local police, I suspect, are in the Mertons' pockets, so why should the locals believe that the Edinburgh police are any different. And those who were prepared to talk gave me the same information that Sid obtained."

"But you were also looking into the people who will be affected by the opening up of the quarry," said Jenkins, "and the subsequent noise and pollution that will inevitably be produced."

"I think it shows the sort of people that the young Mertons were," I told them, "that they only announced a few weeks ago to those who would be affected, that a quarry was going to be opened. This was after they had done all the negotiations with the quarry company in secret. So they were presenting a *fait accompli* to these people. There was still the trivial matter of getting planning permission but that was a trifle since most, if not all, of the members of the Planning Committee are likely to do what the Mertons tell them to do."

"But there was a committee formed to protest at what had been done and to try to reverse the decision, wasn't there?" asked Fletcher.

"There was," I agreed. "Apart from the professional protesters who always come out of the woodwork when what they regard as a just cause appears, the majority of the committee consisted of people who were going to be badly affected, in one way or another, by the work of the quarry."

"Weren't people going to be thrown out of their homes to make way for the access road?" quizzed Beaumont.

"These people didn't have much of a beef," I suggested. "They are goin g to be given what are probably nicer new homes than the ones they have lost, in a more desirable area and will receive reasonable compensation to cover the costs of the move. It was the people who are located right next to where the quarry will be who were up in arms. They would have to put up with lots of noise from the quarry and from the lorries coming and going with the stone. The children will also be at hazard from all the traffic that will be produced and may have to be kept in the house at all times. In addition, there is likely to be a large amount of pollution from the dust that would be continually thrown up. And these people are to get no compensation."

"So are any of the protesters liable to try to murder the members of the Merton family who caused this to happen?" asked Jenkins.

"The most vocal of the protesters is a man who lives in one of the affected cottages, called Ewan Grant. He has a son who suffers from asthma and Grant is worried as to what effect all the dust produced could have on his son. He works in one of the local factories, drinks a lot of a weekend and is liable to lose his temper easily when he has too much whisky in him.  He has a few convictions for assault.  He has been issuing threats as to what he would do to the Mertons while in his cups, so he is certainly one whom we must keep an eye on."

"So what are the tasks for each of us for tomorrow?" asked Jenkins.

"We will do blanket jobs on each of our new suspects.  Andy will take MacCallum, Sid will have Mathers and you will look into Grant.  These are, as far as I can see, the most likely of our suspect. I will take as my chore two of the more marginal suspects, this fellow just out of prison, Goff, and MacTavish. Andy will also see if anything more can be found out about what Basil Douglas actually did after he left the dance last night. But we should all be keeping an ear open for anything being said about any of the suspects. If we don't get back earlier from these enquiries, we will meet here after five."

As Fletcher went off to fetch another round of

drinks, Beaumont asked the question that all of us had been waiting for.

"Has Forsyth made any interesting observations about the murder?"

"He seemed concerned about the fact that two panes of glass had been removed from the French window and not just one," I told him.

"I suppose it does seem an unnecessary thing to do," mused Andy. "And you don't do anything unnecessary when you are breaking into a house in the middle of the night to kill someone. Any ideas as to why the second pane was taken out?"

"Not a clue," I admitted. "I suppose it's easier to fish out the key when you have more room in which to work. But is the extra time taken to remove the second pane, which makes the possibility of discovery more likely, really worth it? I would doubt it. Has anyone any interesting suggestions?"

It was naturally Malcolm Jenkins who was prepared to put forward an idea in order to show to all of us that he was the up and coming man.

"If two people were involved, it might be easier for them to manipulate a pole between them in order to get the key. And that would require that they opened up a second pane for the second person."

"I haven't actually thought about two people being involved," I admitted, "apart from the possibility of Harriet Merton and Callum Douglas working in concert, and they wouldn't need two people fishing for the key since Harriet could get a hold of it without any effort. Have you any suggestions as to whom the pair you are suggesting are involved in the break-in might be?"

"I still think that it is too simplistic to believe that the feud between the Mertons and the Douglases, which has been going on for centuries, has suddenly diminished to nothing. The pair could well have been the two Douglas sons."

"But Harriet Merton claims that Callum was with her at the time of the killing," objected Beaumont. "Why should she lie about that? And why should she give an alibi to someone who might be the person who killed her brother?"

"Callum might have been stringing her along all this time in order to find out what was going on in the Merton household," suggested Jenkins, "if he and Basil had contemplated this killing for some time. And, if she is madly in love with him, she might well give him an alibi if he told her that he was worried that the police might try to pin the murder on him, as a Douglas and therefore a hater of the Mertons, if he wasn't able to convince them that he had been elsewhere."

We sat and thought about it. Eventually, since no-one else seemed inclined to say anything, I gave him my verdict.

"There are a hell of a lot of assumptions in that scenario, most of which I personally don't believe to be likely. But, since Forsyth seems worried about the two panes and yours is the only reason for it that we have come up with, perhaps that is what he is thinking about. And we haven't so many good theories that we can afford to dismiss any suggestion. It is possible that you are right, so we will keep your theory in reserve. And you can add to your duties for tomorrow an attempt to find if Callum was seen out and about at the time when he was supposed to be ensconced in the cottage getting it pff with Harriet."

"Was there anything else that Forsyth seemed worried about?"

"Anyone know anything about knots?" I asked.

There was a general shaking of heads. I put on the table four photo enlargements of the knot on the rope with which Merton's wrists had been tied. They all craned to look at it.

"Nobody, including Forsyth, seemed to know what kind of knot it is. If we could decide what sort of person would use a knot like that, it could give us a clue to the killer. I have had a look at an encyclopaedia that shows all sorts of knots but that one wasn't in it. We will each take one of these photos and, if you know anyone who is into knots, let them have a look to see if they recognise it."

We broke up shortly after that, Jenkins and I making tracks for home. Beaumont and Fletcher, both of whose wives had left them, stayed on, ordering food and more drinks. A congenial session in the pub would look a lot better to each of them than a takeaway in front of the tele.

After a pleasant meal, washed down with an interesting but unpretentious Chianti in an Italian restaurant on the way to Liberton, which is in the south of the city and is the location where I park my weary bones after work, I spent an evening going over the case without getting any brilliant ideas that might lead to a solution and then had an undisturbed sleep.

# CHAPTER 4

I suppose that it might be appropriate for me now to give a little more information about the two main characters in the story, namely Forsyth and myself. He is an imposing figure, an adjective that can also be applied to the way in which he deals with the hired help. He is 6' 4" with a large-boned, quite athletic frame which he keeps in reasonable nick with exercise and golf. A shock of blonde hair stands up above the broad forehead that crowns his long, rather distinguished face and a luxuriant moustache adorns, to be kind about it, his upper lip.

Forsyth's origins are somewhat obscure though I gather that he was born somewhere in the Highlands to a reasonably well-off family, but that he was educated at an exclusive public school in Edinburgh and then at the University there. What qualification he finished up with, I don't know, but I would expect it to have been a first class honours degree in something like the old-style Mathematics and Natural Philosophy Arts course. That would be consistent with both his logical mind and the fact that he is interested in, and very well read in, the Arts. He was married at quite an early age but the union didn't turn out too well and ended in a very acrimonious divorce. This unpleasant ending to the marriage may explain his secretiveness and his unwillingness to leave himself open to criticism or to be shown to be in the wrong in any matter. He now lives alone, very well looked after by a housekeeper who is not only competent but an excellent cook. He enjoys a social life that includes golf at one of the more exclusive courses, bridge at one of the local clubs in Edinburgh, concerts and the theatre, and that allows him to mix with the great and the good in the higher echelons of Edinburgh society. We don't see all that much of him outside working hours though we are invited round to his house in a fairly exclusive area of Edinburgh for dinner from time to time and are always well looked after, superbly fed and supplied with a sufficiency of excellent wine and spirits.

It is not clear why Forsyth chose the police force as a career. He would have succeeded at almost any job he had decided to pursue. It is also difficult to imagine how he endured the years as a humble footslogger without resigning in frustration or being thrown out on his ear by outraged superiors, or how he ever achieved promotion to his present elevated rank. It is probable that in these days he had not yet acquired his later arrogance and was more prepared to conform and to turn that massive intellect to trivial and uninspiring tasks. Legend has it that one of his more perceptive superiors recognised his qualities and took the trouble to steer him gently through the troubled waters to his present safe and well-fitting niche. Stories abound of the sudden flashes of genius from him that illuminated the impenetrable dark of difficult cases, endearing him to the high and mighty and leading to his elevation but I doubt that his rise from the ranks happened that way and I strongly suspect that most of the examples quoted are apocryphal.

It says much for the Lothian and Borders Police that they are prepared to put up with a Chief Inspector who is bored by ninety per cent of his job and, in consequence, is worse than useless at it, in order to have him available when the other ten per cent appears on the scene. I suppose that it also says much for the squads whom he has commanded that they are also prepared to put up with him. Not that those at the bottom of the pile in any police force have much say in their fate. Though those of us who work under him often resent being landed with jobs he should be doing as well as our own, and spend a good deal of our time taking the mickey when he's at his most infuriating or arrogant, we would defend him to the death against any outsider. He has pulled too many chestnuts out of the fire for us in the past and, despite the appalling conceit of the man in assuming that we will be delighted to do, without a murmur of dissent, all the hard graft he should be tackling himself, we know that he has fought for us when we have got into trouble and always makes sure that we share in the credit when he has cracked one of the big ones. We have a real love-hate relationship with the man but no-one has ever asked to be shifted from his squad.

As for me, I was born in Edinburgh and spent my early years in a tenement flat off Dundee Street. My father worked in a nearby brewery, of which Edinburgh at that time had more than its fair share, but he was killed in an accident at work when I was just eight years old. The firm did well by us according to their lights and the mores of the times. They gave the family a tiny pension and my mother a job serving food to the bosses in their canteen. As a result, we managed to live reasonably comfortable lives in comparison with many others in the area though money was always a bit on the tight side. And, since I was now the orphaned son of an Edinburgh burgess, I was eligible to become a Foundationer at George Heriot's School.

George Heriot, Jinglin' Geordie as Sir Walter Scott called him in his novel, was a goldsmith in the reign of James VI of Scotland. He made a pretty good living at his craft, but an even better one from lending money to the King and the courtiers who were always in need of a ready source of cash. When the sovereign became James 1 of the newly formed Great Britain and moved to London, Heriot went with him. Since the need for ready money was even greater there for a king and nobles living well beyond their means, Geordie found himself coining in the readies hand over fist. Since he had no heirs when he died, he left his money to found a school for the orphans of the Edinburgh citizenry.

The trustees were shrewd Scots businessmen who invested the money wisely. The Trust grew and prospered. More than a century ago the school expanded and opened its doors to all the sons of Edinburgh who could afford the fees, the Foundationers no longer boarding in the school building but receiving an allowance to stay elsewhere and attend the school, like the rest, as day pupils. I was one of these, staying at home with my mother during the night but mixing with the sons of the well-to-do middle classes on an equal footing during the day. I acquired not only a sound education but an insight into a life far removed from that of my mother. She had always been a great reader and, from her, I had acquired a love of literature. At Heriot's I added a liking for good music and the theatre. While I did well enough in exams, I was never one of the high flyers. Although I was urged by some of the teachers to go on to university and take a degree, I knew that wasn't for me. Book learning I had had enough of. I wanted some hands-on experience. I was keen to go on learning, but in a job.

What led me to a career in the police I'm not sure. Perhaps it was the great respect for the law that my mother dinned into me. Or perhaps it was the lawlessness that I saw, and hated, in the jungle of tenements around where I lived. Since my mother refused point blank to leave the flat in which she had spent so much of her life and near which all her friends resided, and I didn't feel that I could desert her, my early years as a copper were not pleasant. My neighbours regarded me as a traitor to my roots and it was always uncomfortable when I was involved in any operation that impinged on the criminal occupations of the area. So, when my mother died, I moved as far away from the area as possible and bought a bungalow in Liberton on the southern side of the city. I still had the odd friend in the district where I'd grown up, but we tended to meet in town on the increasingly fewer occasions on which we got together. When you're in the police and have come from a poor background, you have to make new friends to survive.

I got a transfer to the CID in due course and never looked back. Detective work proved to be my metier. I had a certain native intelligence and worked hard. I passed the sergeants' exams and got promoted. I hadn't been long a sergeant when I was informed that I was to be installed in Forsyth's squad, his previous sergeant having at last made it to the rank of Inspector, leaving behind a vacancy that had to be filled. I was initially flattered to be assigned to the team of a man with the kind of reputation that Forsyth had, since he was, even then, a bit of a legend, although I had heard that he could be a difficult man to work for. I soon found out that working for him was not likely to be a bed of roses and I was already somewhat disillusioned when the first murder case in which we were involved together came along. It was a pretty traumatic experience where the way in which Forsyth conducted the investigation almost gave me heart failure and where I feared at one time that my career in the police force was about to come to an ignominious end. I have chronicled these never-to-be-forgotten events in a story entitled *The Crime Committee.* Fortunately, it turned out all right in the end, Forsyth solved the case brilliantly, winning some excellent wine in the process, which he shared with the rest of us, and we became an established team.

These traumatic events that formed the

beginning of our work as a team explain the odd relationship that I have with Forsyth. When you have seen Forsyth at his best and also at his worst, totally ignoring the rules of how a crime should be investigated, you find yourself a little short in the tugging of the forelock mentality.

# CHAPTER 5

The next morning, I called at Headquarters in Fettes first thing in order to apprise Forsyth of the results of all the enquiries that the team had made and which they had reported to me the previous evening. He absorbed the information and sat for some time without making any comment on it.

There seemed no harm in seeing if he would give me any hint of the direction in which his instincts were leading him, so I asked if any of what he had just heard had seemed to lead us further along the road to the truth. But I might have known that he was too wily to fall for such an obvious ploy.

"Why don't you give me an assessment of your view of the likelihood of each suspect being our murderer," he replied, "and I will then comment on whether your assessment agrees with my own."

I supposed that that was better than nothing.

"I can't see the Douglases," I said at length, "in this day and age trying to kill off the Mertons because of an ancient feud. But I can see Harriet

Merton as the killer. She is on the plain side and it would certainly make a marked improvement in her prospects of getting a husband if she was the heir to a wealthy estate. And I can see Callum Douglas making up to her and encouraging her to kill off her brothers if that would not only make an end to the feud but make her a very tempting catch. And, although it seems less likely, Basil Douglas might be encouraging his brother to spur Harriet on if that led to the two estates being combined."

"That seems a fair assessment," he conceded. "So we keep Harriet as a chief suspect with the others only involved as accessories."

"As to the plebs, I would regard MacCallum, Mathers and Grant as the most likely to fill the role of murderer. The motives of MacTavish and Goff seem a trifle too slim to make them resort to murder, preceded by torture."

"Fair enough. But we should not lose sight of them in consequence. What makes a man want revenge might often seem quite trivial to the rest of us saner mortals."

"And which of that lot," I asked, "would you regard as the one to put money on?"

He brushed that one aside easily.

"It is much too early to have favourites. At this stage, we have not enough evidence."

. I left him and departed to begin my investigation of Goff and MacTavish. This took me the rest of the day and I was feeling in need of a comfortable sit down and a long drink, indeed more than one, when I entered the pub to find Beaumont and Fletcher already there at our usual table with, as expected, pints of heavy in front of them. Jenkins came in while I was at the bar, so I added to my order of a pint of heavy for me a gin and tonic for him. We took our drinks over to join the other two, greeted them, sat down and I took a long and refreshing swallow of the beer.

"I badly needed that," I said. "It's been a long and tedious day. I am sure you all found the same. So let's hear how you all got on and what insights into the case you have managed to achieve. Andy, why don't you start the ball rolling."

He had a quick swallow of beer and started on his account.

"MacCallum is a big, well-built man who makes his presence felt and is not afraid to do so. He ran the Merton Arms until he was kicked out. According to what I gathered from the locals, he was quite a popular landlord though perhaps inclined to throw his weight around a bit as one of the influential people in Auchenbland. He was also a leading figure in the local Business Men's Association and on the Town Council, though neither organisation was ever able to do anything that the Mertons disapproved of. But he obviously wasn't doing everything that the Mertons expected of him because he was thrown out without warning when they had their big overhaul of who deserved to have the shops and houses in the town. He now works behind the bar in one of the pubs in Auchenbland on what will be pretty minimum wages, so that his income will have crashed along with his status in the community."

"So does he feel so badly done by," asked Fletcher, "that he's likely to be popping off the Mertons who caused his ruin?"

"He had his son in a private school and was forced to pull him out of there and send him to the local comprehensive. And there, since the place has had a series of bad reviews, not only is he getting an inferior education, but he has been subjected to some pretty serious bullying. The effect of all that on his son's future prospects is one of the items that rankles most with MacCallum and, along with his lack of status, might in time have caused him to start on a murderous trail of revenge."

"Did you find out what he was doing at the time of the killing?"

"He wasn't seen by anyone out and about that night, though that doesn't mean anything. If he was careful, he would keep out of anyone's way. He was supposed to have been at home, as he usually is at night but, since his wife was away staying with her elderly mother, he hasn't even got her to confirm his alibi."

"So he stacks up as a good prospect for the killer," I said thoughtfully. "Did you find out any more about Basil Douglas and where he was after the dance on the night of Ralph's death?"

"He still maintains stoutly that he spent the whole night with the girl with whom he left the dance, while she insists that they parted at her door. It comes down to his word against hers. They both seem perfectly capable of lying for their own ends. But I can't see why he would have claimed he was with her if he knew she would deny it. I wouldn't put it past her to have demanded some reward for backing up his perfectly true story and he is the sort of man who would not stand for blackmail and who would tell her to go jump in the lake."

"Right. So we have to leave that for the moment to see how it will resolve itself. What did you find out about Mathers, Sid?"

"Bill Mathers," Fletcher informed us, "is a

perfectly ordinary fellow who ran the grocer's shop in the High Street of Auchenbland and was a member of the Business Men's Association and had been a captain of the Bowls Club. His wife was prominent in the Women's Institute. So the family were well regarded in the upper strata of the town's society. I gather that Mathers gave credit in his shop, and almost certainly lent money on the side, no doubt at exorbitant rates of interest. That may be one of the reasons why the Mertons got rid of him during the purge. His father had had the grocer's shop before him and it had always been assumed that he would take over when his father retired. He was not very academically inclined and had acquired no qualifications so, when he found himself out of a job, he was unable to get another one and has spent the time since then on the dole. The family now live in the slummier part of town and their son has acquired a drug habit. The daughter is a member of a gang and has already had to have an abortion. Mrs Mathers has found it difficult to adjust to her new life and has had a bit of a breakdown. Mathers himself drinks too much."

"And the drink," observed Jenkins, "might give him the courage to go out to get revenge for the horrible life into which he and his family have been plunged, by eliminating the two people who have caused it."

"And Mathers was not at home on the night of the killing," Fletcher informed us. "He had been drinking in his local pub and claims that he had had too much of the stuff and passed out in an alleyway on his trip home. But no-one claims to have seen him lying stoned in any of the town's lanes."

"So, another good possibility as our assassin," I suggested. "Can you eliminate Grant as a suspect, Malcolm?"

"I'm not sure that I can," said Jenkins. "He is a smallish man but very tough. He is incensed that the Mertons did the deal with the quarry company in secret, leaving the people affected little time to organise a protest. And he is particularly worried about the possible effects that the dust from the workings will have on his son, who is in a pretty bad way as it is without this added pollution. He is a man who drinks a lot and is liable to get quite aggressive when he was had too much and he is crossed. He has issued threats as to what he was going to do to the Mertons to make them pay for what they were about to subject his son to. I could see him putting these threats into effect if he had absorbed a skinful. And his claim is that he was at home at the time of the murder. But the only person who can confirm that is his wife. And, since she is against the Mertons as much he is, that is not a great alibi."

"So another good prospect," I said.

I got my thoughts together since it was now my turn to report on the day's findings.

"As to MacTavish," I began, "perhaps he is not as good a prospect as the others, but he can't be ruled out. He is a tall, thin man who lived in a nice house with a wife and a kid. He liked a drink from time to time and was very noisily obstreperous and belligerent when he had had too much. So there had been a few complaints made against him and that may have been why he was evicted in the purge. The only accommodation he could get was pretty slummy and his wife was not amused and very soon left him for someone with better prospects, taking the kid with her. That merely increased his drinking and he has issued threats on more than one occasion when in his cups against the Mertons who, he maintains, caused all his troubles. He has a history of violence when crossed when he is drunk, so one can't rule out the possibility of him doing the Mertons when drunk and angry, but I think that he may well be so far down the slippery slope that he is no longer in a state to do anything that serious. He was drinking on the evening of the murder, left the pub in a belligerent mood and was not seen again until late the next morning. So he may well have made his way up to the big house and killed Ralph."

I picked up my glass and had a soothing drink before resuming.

"Are you going to add Goff to the list or can you eliminate him?" asked Beaumont.

"Goff ran a garage in the town," I explained, "and was good at spotting the fault in a car. He was generally highly thought of. He had been President of the local cricket club and also the Chairman of the angling club that used the local river. He had been known as a fast driver and it didn't come as a great surprise to the town when he was accused of knocking down and killing a child, though most people were sure that he would have stopped if he had known that he had hit anyone. So people accepted the Merton version that he had probably been unaware of what he had done. He had a wife and a little girl and they had a poor time while he was in gaol. Now that he's out again, he has a job in a garage and is looking to take over and run one in the future. Since he got out, he hasn't expressed any resentment towards the Mertons about them telling on him but he might be suppressing that for obvious reasons. He was allegedly at home asleep on the night of Ralph's murder. Whether his wife would lie for him if he wasn't there all night, I wouldn't know. But she probably would. She has stuck with him throughout his troubles and seems very loyal to him."

I took another deep draught of beer and looked around at the team.

"We have a fair number of good suspects. They are Harriet Merton, Callum Douglas, or Harriet and Callum working in concert. Basil Douglas, MacCallum, Mathers, MacTavish, Grant and Goff. They all could have done it, since none of them has an alibi that stands up to serious scrutiny and all have motives, some better than others. But I don't see what we can do to pin the crime on any of them unless someone now comes forward and says that he saw one or other of them creeping stealthily about on the night of the killing."

They thought about it while Jenkins went off to fetch another round. It was he who made the first comment when he returned.

"I go for Basil," he said. "The fact that he

thought that he had persuaded one of his girlfriends to give him an alibi and she has now very sensibly decided not to get mixed up in attempts to fool the police strikes me as very significant. The Mertons and the Douglases have been at each other's throats for centuries. I don't buy it being any different in these modern times whatever they may say. And, of course, he may be aware that his brother and Harriet Merton have got together. With the two Merton sons out of the way, Harriet inherits and, if the two lovebirds get married, Basil can see the two estates being merged eventually with an enormous increase in his influence in the region."

There was a pause before Beaumont came in. Jenkins was not his favourite policeman, since he regarded him as pushy. And, since he himself had no ambition to get further up the ladder, he regarded Jenkins as far too ambitious, and he was always suspicious of graduates, particularly if they were on fast track promotion schemes. I was not surprised to find that he would take an opposing view.

"I disagree. I think that two feuding families murdering each other to increase their influence in this day and age is fantasy. I think it much more likely that one of the people kicked out by the Mertons from their livelihood or their home is seeking revenge. That is the sort of motive for murder that doesn't change with the times and is always there."

I had expected Jenkins to fly to the defence of his theory but he merely shrugged and held his peace. No doubt he felt it a waste of time to argue about matters when there was no evidence for or against any theory. There was another silence before Fletcher felt that he should say something. But he is never the greatest of thinkers and clearly didn't have a serious view.

"On the basis that the least unlikely solution is often the correct one in a classic detective story," he said. "I go for Goff."

"You've got it wrong," retorted Beaumont. "It isn't the least likely suspect that turns out to be the murderer in an Agatha Christie story, it is the person who hasn't even been suspected. So you should have gone for someone like Fisher who will turn out to be the illegitimate son of old man Merton, a theory that will become more obvious when Harriet is chopped as well, so that the bastard can inherit."

And that exchange brought an end to the discussion. From then on we talked on other matters before breaking up.  As on the previous night, Jenkins and I left while the other two put in orders for food and stayed.

I had not been in long the next morning when Sergeant Anderson from the desk phoned me and told me that there had been a fire up at the Merton country seat, which was rated to be a case of arson. Since that might be connected to the previous murder, it had been decided that the Forsyth team should investigate.  I sent the others off to get things started and went to advise Forsyth that he would be unable to skulk in his office that day but would have to venture out into the big, wide world.

We didn't have much conversation on the drive

to the Merton home, each of us no doubt trying to tie this latest development in with what we had already discovered about the murder. At the house, we found Andy Beaumont awaiting us in the parking area and, after the usual greetings, he guided us round to the back of the house, explaining what had happened as we went.

"At about three this morning, someone sneaked into the grounds, came up to the house and removed a pane of glass from a window in one of the wings at the back that's used mainly for recreation and storage and so is not occupied at night," he told us. "Then he or she seems to have poured petrol in and set it alight. Fortunately, the Mertons have a good fire alarm system, so the household was quickly aroused and they were able to put the fire out. The wing is badly damaged but at least the fire didn't get to spread to other parts of the house."

"So, having killed the two sons, our killer now wants to finish off the rest of the family by incinerating them," I suggested.

"It looks that way," said Andy.

There was a forensic team examining what remained after the fire.  One of them told us that it was definitely arson but that they had found nothing that was likely to lead them to the identity of the person who had caused the conflagration.

We went into the house and found old Mr Merton in a state of fury.

"They not only kill my two sons but now they try to get rid of the rest of the family in one go.  When are you going to arrest the Douglases and mete out the punishment that they deserve?"

"There is no evidence that the Douglases either started the fire or were responsible for the killing of your sons," said Forsyth mildly.

"Of course they committed all these crimes," yelled Merton furiously. "Who else would do such things but them?"

"The Mertons are not overpopular ín Auchenbland," I pointed out.  "There are a number of people there  who think  that they have  been treated somewhat badly by you and your sons and some of them have been heard to issue threats against your family."

"The townsfolk," he said contemptuously. "They wouldn't dare."

"They would, you know. This is no longer the middle ages."

He continued to maintain that the Douglases were responsible and we could get no more that was sensible out of him. Harriet was no help in getting to the culprits since she claimed that she was baffled as to why the fire had been started.

We had a good look round but could find nothing that indicated who was responsible for the crime. Fletcher and Jenkins appeared and reported that no-one had been observed anywhere near the house nor grounds at the relevant time during the night.

There seemed no point in staying there and, having instructed the team to make enquiries as to the whereabouts of all our suspects early that morning, I drove Forsyth back to Edinburgh. On the drive, I tried to find out if the fire had led him to decrease the odds on any of the suspects.

"It has not," he replied. "Has it done so for you?"

"Harriet and the Douglases," I suggested, "would have no interest in burning the family seat to the ground. So it looks as if one of the disgruntled plebs is to blame. And I suppose my money would be on Grant, since he is becoming desperate and getting rid of the whole clan at one swoop might be the only way to stop the quarry development."

"But did the person who started the fire really wish to burn the house, and all its occupants, to the ground?" he asked.

I looked at him in surprise.

"What are you suggesting?"

"If I wanted to burn the Mertons, the house and their possessions to the ground, I would start the fire in the main building and not in one of the wings, particularly one that contained little that would fuel the fire. Indeed, I would prepare several fires and set them off simultaneously. In that way the family might well have been trapped in the house and unable to get out. In addition, it is unlikely that they could have put out the fire and saved the house from destruction as they were quite easily able to do when only one wing was involved."

I was impressed. The thought had not occurred to me.

"So it looks as if it might be Harriet or her lover who might have been responsible. Starting a fire, that wasn't going to do much real damage and could easily be put out, would nonetheless remove possible suspicions that we might have regarding their involvement in the death of the brothers."

"It is certainly one possible scenario," he said judiciously. He looked at me with a mischievous grin on his face. "Someone certainly wished the Mertons to be 'frighted with false fire'."

I accepted the challenge and thought about it. Eventually I got it.

"Hamlet, I think."

"You are doing well," he said in congratulation.

We drove for the rest of the way in silence while I thought about his theory about the reason for the fire being started. And, the more I thought about it, the more I liked the idea.

I spent the rest of the day trying to find out what I could about the Mertons and the Douglases, their interrelations and where they had all been at the times of the murder of Ralph and of the fire. But nothing that I learned took me any further forward. So I dropped in to the local cop shop to have a word with the man who ran it, Sergeant Walter Dalrymple. He was a slim man, getting on in years, with a hatchet face under a mass of brown hair, now turning white. I had been told that he was a man contented with his lot who seemed perfectly happy to spend the rest of his career in this backwater. I told him that we had a number of suspects for the murders of the two Merton boys and that it would be useful if he, a man who would know all of them intimately because of his job, told me what he knew of them and gave me his opinion as to how likely he regarded them to be killers. I told him the list of names that we had come up with.

Dalrymple looked at me speculatively and thought for a while before replying.

"I have heard that you and Inspector Forsyth make a good team and that you are honest coppers, so I will tell you what I ken about that lot. Harriet from the big house is, like her brothers were, ruthless and self-centred, so I would not put it past her to make a bid for the Merton estate. But you would have to be pretty sick to kill your own brothers.

"The Douglases are a bad lot but I dinna think that the old feud that exists would be enough to have them killing Mertons out of the blue for no good reason. So there would have to be some incident that started the present stramash and I havena heard of anything."

"These are very helpful comments," I suggested. "So it looks as if you would put your money on one of the locals."

He ignored my comment.

"MacCallum was no a bad landlord although he gave himself a few airs and graces that were no justified and he ran the Business Man's Club well when he has the chairman. And he ran the hotel fine as well and felt hard done by when he was kicked out. And he has had a hard time since then. And he's a man who nurses grudges.

"Mathers was a bit on the slimy side for my taste. He reminded me a lot of Uriah Heep. And he lent money to his customers, which he wasn't licensed to do, and charged quite a high interest. But I could never do anything about that side of his business because the people who made use of his service valued it and wouldn't testify agin him."

When he paused, I came in.

"So do you reckon him as a killer?"

"He probably deserved to be thrown out of his shop for his money-lending activities, but he wouldn't see it that way. And, since he is the sort of man to resent any insult, real or imagined, done to him, it's no unlikely that he might seek his revenge."

"And MacTavish?"

"I'd no rate him highly as a suspect. Since he lost his fine house, he has gone downhill rapidly. I wouldn't think him capable of doing anything seriously violent unless he was full of the drink and in a belligerent mood.

"Goff is a different proposition. He has the resolution and determination to do anything, but I do not see that he has sufficient of a quarrel with the Mertons to drive him to murder. He is well liked here. He is a fine left-handed batsman who opens the innings for the local team. His problem is that he drives too fast and sometimes after having a drink. He was stopped and found to be over the limit twice before the accident, so it didn't come as a great surprise when he was sent down."

"So that leaves only Grant."

"And he is a grand prospect," said the sergeant. "He has fine grounds for being angry with the Mertons. They pulled a bit of a fast one by doing all the negotiations with the quarry people in real secrecy. But he is a man with a violent temper and he drinks too much and gets his mind enraged when the whisky is in him. His son is the apple of his eye and he rightly fears what the dust from the new operation will do to his asthma. I wouldn't put anything past him where his son's welfare is at stake."

We sat back and I thought about what he had said. I liked the man and he seemed to be someone who could take a bit of a ribbing.

"Maybe there is one more suspect we should consider," I said lightly.

"And who would that be?" he asked.

"A local policeman," I suggested.

"Indeed. And why would he be interested in getting rid of the odd Merton?"

"It must be a bit frustrating running the local nick," I pointed out. "If anything you feel it necessary to do conflicts with the Merton interests, one of them will be on the phone to your immediate superior, with the result that you are told to back off and not disturb the peaceful waters. A man who has suffered in this way for years may eventually decide to do something to show that he can still make his own decisions. And such a man would know how to ensure that no clues were left behind for the detectives."

"I like it," he replied with a smile on his face. "I can see why you and Inspector Forsyth have something of a reputation. You think outside the box. Would you do me the honour of having a drink with me in the local pub before you decide to arrest me?"

A proposition to which I gladly agreed. He had struck me as an old time copper of a vintage that no longer existed. I enjoyed his pawky humour over a couple of pints of beer.

# CHAPTER 6

When I got back to Fettes, I told the rest of the team about Forsyth's suggestion about the nature and purpose of the fire. They also were impressed. We discussed the matter at length but reached no shattering conclusion. I also gave them Dalrymple's take on the likelihood of the various suspects being our murderer. But we had little further to discuss and the meeting didn't last long.

After dinner, I had a night off from thinking about the murders, instead watching some mindless television programmes.

I had just got in and was settled behind my desk the following morning when Sergeant Anderson from the front desk informed me that another death had occurred, this time in the town of Auchenbland and that Forsyth and his team had better go out there, nab the fellow who was responsible for all these dreadful killings and put a stop to the slaughter of the innocents, or indeed the guilty, before the whole of the population of the area was wiped out.

"Who has been killed this time?" I asked.

"A fellow by the name of Dan Inglis."

The name didn't ring a bell. Had we been barking up the wrong tree all along?

"Who the hell is Dan Inglis?"

"He apparently was the landlord of the Merton Arms."

Memory flooded back. Inglis was the new tenant who had taken over from MacCallum when the latter had been given his marching orders. And it struck me immediately that this further death seemed utterly logical if the ousted landlord was the person who was doing all the killings.

I sent out to the murder scene the three other members of the team who were to get enquiries started and then I waited for Forsyth to arrive at Headquarters. When he did put in an appearance, I apprised him of the new development.

"How appropriate," he said and then quoted, "An inn, a place not to live but to die in."

He looked at me quizzically. I thought long and

hard as we proceeded to my car to get out to Auchenbland, but eventually had to confess myself beaten.

"Not very well known, so don't feel discouraged." he said in a kindly voice. "William Browne, a writer who lived and wrote in the seventeenth and eighteenth centuries."

Once we were on our way, I thought it worthwhile to find out if the latest murder fitted in with whatever his thinking had been, as it seemed to fit with one of the theories that we had been expounding in the pub, namely the one that assumed that MacCallum was responsible.

"As you will no doubt be aware," I said, "the team has been discussing the case and we have come up with a number of suspects. The latest death seems to fit in nicely with one of the theories that has been advanced and so is not unexpected. Do you also find it logical that this death has occurred?"

He took a little time before replying. He never

likes to say anything about a case that might give a clue to his thinking until he is quite sure that he has the correct answer. This allows him, if his original thinking was wrong, to retain his reputation for being infallible. And, if the original thinking was correct, the fact that we have got no inkling of his reasoning makes the impact of the revelation of his final solution all the more impressive.

He finally admitted to me somewhat grudgingly that what little evidence there had been that had pointed to anyone after the first murder had not led him to anticipate the death of Mr Inglis.

Forsyth would never openly lie to me but he might well try to mislead. I was not sure whether he was being a little too literal and trying to put me off the scent because he had come to the same conclusion as to the reason for the Inglis murder as I had, or whether he had genuinely been looking for the killer in a totally different direction from the team.

"Surely it's too much of a coincidence for the murder of Inglis not to be directly connected to the other two," I suggested.

A curious expression appeared on his face.

"The long arm of coincidence," he quoted in a rather abstracted voice.

"Not a quotation I know," I had to admit.

"Haddon Chambers," he said, still immersed in thought. "An Australian who came to England and became a successful playwright." There was a pause and then, after a few moments a smile appeared on his face and he beamed at me.

"Coincidence," he said cheerfully. "You are, as always, invaluable in bringing important matters to my attention. Now that you have got my mind into the right mould, I see that what you have said is perfectly correct. This murder is a logical progression from the other two."

So he was thinking along the same lines as the team, though why he had not seen immediately that the death of Inglis fitted perfectly into the scheme of things I found difficult to understand

We rode for the rest of the journey in silence,

each absorbed in his own thoughts. When we arrived in Auchenbland, I parked in the car park of the Merton Arms which, by this time, contained a large number of vehicles. When we entered the building, Beaumont was there to greet us as usual.

"Morning, sir," he said to the Chief. "The dead man's name is Dan Inglis. He is the tenant of this place and has been for just over a year since the Mertons made a change in several of the tenancies. Before that, he ran a small pub on the outskirts of the town. So getting this place was quite a step up. By all accounts he was well liked and no-one, as far as is known, had a grudge against him. He is a bachelor who lives here on his own at nights, so that he was not found until the first employee arrived and eventually went to look for him when he didn't appear. He has been killed in the same manner as Ralph Merton was, although it looks as if he wasn't taken while he was asleep. The murderer gained access to the building via a toilet window where the catch is loose."

Where the loose catches existed in a hotel was something that would be well known to a former tenant, I noted.

"We had better have a look at the body," observed the Chief.

Beaumont conducted us through the public areas of the inn to the private quarters behind. They seemed quite luxurious and the bedroom into which we were directed was comfortably furnished. The body of Inglis lay naked on the bed, the covers, a pillow and the publican's pyjamas having been thrown down on the floor. It was obvious that the dead man had been subjected to a considerable amount of torture before he had been put out of his misery. His limbs were in contorted positions, there were burn marks and savage cuts all over his body and tape had been stuck across his mouth to contain his screams.

But, as Andy had said, Inglis had not been asleep when the killer had broken in. He had clearly heard the intruder and had tried to phone for help.

But the killer had wrenched the phone connection from the wall, thrown the instrument aside to where it lay in a corner of the room and then attacked Inglis. There had been a bit of a struggle with a chair and a stool being knocked over and several items had been swept off the dressing table. But eventually Inglis had been knocked unconscious, after which the killer had stripped the body, put it back on the bed, tied it up, fastened tape across the mouth and proceeded to the torturing of his victim.

Doc Hay had been standing lost in thought by the body when we entered the room, but he came over to greet us when he saw that we had arrived on the scene.

"I should guess that we have here the same sadistic killer that did in the Merton boy," he told us. "The murder is the same in all respects as the other one, except that Inglis was awake when the killer entered. But Inglis was subdued, bashed over the head to keep him quiet while he was tied up and the tape put over his mouth. Then he was tortured, bones broken, many parts of his body burned and his flesh cut. The only difference this time is that the killer took away the rope with which the arms and legs had been tied."

"I wonder why he bothered to do that this time," I murmured.

"He may have had to buy some new rope," suggested Beaumont, "since he left the last lot behind, and may have been worried that we could identify where it was bought."

"You may be right even if he was worrying unnecessarily. But it would be worth checking with any shops that sell rope in the area as to whether any has been purchased recently and by whom. The shopkeepers around here will know most of the locals and will be able to identify the buyer even if they don't know his name."

"You will also want to know that he died about two to three am," Hay added. " And, if there are no questions, I will be off to my next assignment. I have a far too full schedule. The powers that be like to keep me busy. They seem to think that, even at my advanced age, I am liable to get up to mischief if my hands are left idle."

Forsyth looked at me expectantly. I felt that I could not disappoint him.

"Isaac Watts and, in a slightly different form, Proverbs," I said.

"Excellent," he exclaimed in mock admiration.

"Showing off our literary skills, are we?" asked Hay. "It's not necessary to try to impress me. I already know that you lot are a cut above the others."

He drew a cigar case from his pocket, took from it one of his foul smelling cheroots, lit it, puffed at it contentedly, picked up his bag and drifted off from the scene.

One of the forensic team was working his magic in a corner of the room. He admitted that so far he had found nothing likely to excite us.

"You will notice," he added, "that a book has been thrown onto the floor. Whether Inglis was reading it in bed and it got knocked down there when he was clobbered by the killer or, having heard the intruder, he pulled it out from the bookcase beside the bed and left it as a clue is for you to decide."

"Has the book been checked by you for prints?" I enquired.

When I was informed that it had been and that only Inglis' prints had been found on it, I picked it up. It was a hard cover edition of 'Mary Poppins' by P L Travers. I showed it to Forsyth.

"Does it suggest anything to you?" I asked.

He thought about it for a few moments.

"I think that it may well be a clue as to the identity of his murderer that was left here for the police by Inglis," he said.

I stared at it blankly. If I was a clue, it was certainly obscure. I could make nothing of it.

We inspected the window by which the killer had gained entry but again found nothing of interest. I think that Forsyth was about to suggest a return to Headquarters when Fletcher rushed in breathlessly and obviously the bearer of tidings, glad or otherwise. But it took him a few moments to get back his breath.

"Jenkins and I," he finally said, "have been going around the area to see if anyone saw or heard anything last night. I have just been approached by a woman called Esther Murray who works in the grocer's shop. When she arrived at the shop this morning, the man who runs the place. Mike Turner, was not there, which was a bit unusual. When he still didn't arrive on the scene, she went up to the place where he lives, which is situated above the shop. There was no sign of him there and everything seemed to be in order, but she was very worried. It is quite unlike him not to be at the shop to open it up and not to let her know if he is going off somewhere. And, since she had heard of the murder of Inglis, she thought that the police ought to know about Turner's disappearance in case it was connected in some way."

"I thought that Turner was married," I said.

"What happened to the wife and kids?"

"They have gone off for a couple of days to visit the wife's mother."

"Is Esther Murray of the opinion that Turner is the one who killed Inglis and has now done a runner?" asked Beaumont.

"I imagine that that is what she had in her mind," Sid admitted.

"That's ridiculous," I suggested. "In the first place, Inglis and Turner are supposed to be the best of pals and have gone around together since their schooldays. Why would he up and do in his best friend at a time when murders are going on all over the place. And, secondly, if he had gone on the run, then he would have been likely to gather up a few things from the flat to take away with him, and missing items Murray would have surely noticed. And, finally, why would Turner want to kill the two Mertons and Inglis? The Mertons allowed him to get a substantial leg up in the world by letting him run the inn and we've heard nothing about any recent quarrel between the grocer and the Mertons or the publican on our round of listening to the local gossip."

"So why has Turner vanished at the very time that Inglis is killed?" enquired Fletcher. "It can't be just a coincidence."

I gave it a little thought.

"Turner must have been out and about at the time that Inglis was being murdered. We know that they were best pals, so that Turner, with his wife away, may even have been coming here. If he saw the killer, that gentleman would realise that the fact would be reported to us as soon as news of the murder got around. The killer couldn't allow that to happen so he grabbed Turner and either has killed him and dumped the body somewhere or he has knocked him out, tied him up and stashed him somewhere to be dealt with later."

I turned to Forsyth who had remained silent during this exchange.

"Don't you think that that is a reasonable

explanation for Turner's disappearance?"

"I would agree that it is a very reasonable explanation," he said. "I think that you should get as many uniforms as you are able to lay your hands on and send them out and about searching the area for the body of Turner or looking in any likely place in which a still live Turner could be hidden away from sight."

I sent Fletcher off to find Jenkins after which the two were to check alibis of all the suspects, particularly MacCallum, and find out if anyone had seen Turner, or anyone else for that matter, out and about near the Merton Arms at any time during the night. I went with Beaumont to the local nick to organise the acquiring of uniforms from it and from three others in the surrounding area. I managed, after a few arguments and freely using the fearsome name of Forsyth, to get a hold of eight bobbies and left them in the charge of Beaumont who would work out the details of the search and make sure that they kept at it.

When I returned to the Merton Arms, I found the great man sitting in a comfortable chair in the residents' lounge drinking a coffee, eating shortbread and looking very pleased with himself.

"Have you been sitting here doing nothing since I left?" I asked accusingly.

"Far from it," he replied. "I have been out and about verifying a number of suppositions that the latest killing had suggested, after your admirable comment had directed my mind in the right direction. I am happy to report that all my imaginings were revealed as correct. I also had a look at a place where I thought that Turner, dead or alive, might have been deposited but there was nothing where I had imagined that he might be."

There was no point in trying to get him to be a little more specific as to what he had been doing and what it was that he had managed to verify. He would, in the nicest possible way, have turned away my questions without in fact answering them. I assumed that he must have been trying to find out if

MacCallum had been seen out and about during the night and, from his satisfied air, he appeared to have been able to do so. I wondered whether Fletcher and Jenkins would be able to find the same eye witness.

I assumed that he would now wish to return to Headquarters but he surprised me by saying that he would like to have a look over Turner's residence before we did so. We walked there, since it wasn't far. The retail shop was on the ground floor and a stair led up from the shop to the private quarters that Turner and his family had occupied. Forsyth and I walked through the shop, followed by the eyes of the interested customers, mounted the stairs and entered the flat by using the key that Esther Murray had provided. The Chief poked around for a bit. But the only thing that I came across that was untoward was that one of the windows was not snibbed. But in a sleepy, neighbourly town like Auchenbland, security was probably not a high priority.

On the drive back to Edinburgh, Forsyth seemed deep in thought. But I felt it right to break into his reverie to find out how we were going to proceed.

"Do you know who it is who has been doing all these murders?"

"I believe that I do," he replied.

"Then are you about to go and have him arrested?" I asked.

"Unfortunately, we do not have the sort of proof that would appeal to the Procurator Fiscal and persuade him to prosecute."

"But, if it is quite obvious to you who the guilty party is, you surely cannot be intending to allow him to get off scot free."

"Perhaps, when the body of Mr Turner comes to light, we may find there the clue that will allow us to take the case to the Procurator Fiscal."

And with that I had to be content. He was, of course, correct. It might be quite obvious to all of us on the team that MacCallum had committed the series of murders that we had been investigating. But Procurator Fiscals are not keen on logic, even when they understand it. They want solid evidence, like fingerprints and bloodstains to put before a jury since such bodies are notoriously unable to get their minds around logical arguments.

I spent the rest of the day making a few enquiries and also racking my brains to see if I could come up with anything that would make the case more acceptable to the Procurator Fiscal, but without a favourable outcome. So, at five o'clock, I wended my way to the pub. I was the first there and was enjoying a soothing pint of heavy when Beaumont and Fletcher arrived together, closely followed by Jenkins. Once they had acquired drinks, sat down at the table and imbibed sufficient liquid to put them in a genial mood. I asked them to report on what they had been able to find out that day.

Beaumont had directed, and taken part in, the police search for Turner. No dead body had been found and no hiding place where a live Turner might be stored had been discovered. He saw no point in continuing the search the next day since any likely place had already been gone over and it would not be practical to go through every house in Auchenbland looking for the missing man. To do it thoroughly, examining every nook and cranny, would require a lot more than eight men and, even with three times that number, would take months. And MacCallum didn't have a big enough house in which to keep Turner and would be far too canny to do so anyway.

Fletcher and Jenkins had verified that none of the suspects had a sustainable alibi, all having claimed to be at home asleep in bed during the entire night. They had not found anyone who had seen or heard anything suspicious around the time of the crime. So, if Forsyth had actually been able to find a witness, my two had failed to match his effort.

Beaumont had also told the pair to go round all the hardware and similar shops in the area, enquiring about purchases of rope. It turned out that none of the suspects had bought rope recently. But MacCallum might well have a stock of old rope or have bought a new supply somewhere outwith the area.

I went through everything that had happened that day. I like to keep any team of mine abreast of all developments in any case in which we are involved. The lowliest detective constable is as likely to be struck by a brilliant idea as the highest inspector. But he is much less likely to get that flash of genius if he is not conversant with all the facts in a case. When I had finished my recital, I took a swallow of beer and then continued.

"On the last two nights, we spent some time discussing the case and came up with a number of possible suspects. These were Harriet Merton, Basil and Callum Douglas, Colin MacCallum, Bill Mathers, Martin Goff and Ewan Grant, not necessarily all equally likely. But the latest murder seems to me to have eliminated all but one of our suspects."

As I took another swallow of beer, Jenkins came in, keen to show that he was as on the ball as I was.

"Why would a Merton or the Douglases want to kill Inglis? It doesn't make sense. And we haven't heard of any bad blood between Inglis and any of Mathers or Goff or Grant."

"But MacCallum," said Beaumont, cutting in smoothly to stop Jenkins hogging the limelight, "will hate Inglis almost as much as he does the Mertons. If Inglis hadn't wanted to take over the Merton Arms, MacCallum might never have been kicked out of the job in the first place. So the new murder makes sense if MacCallum is the killer, but no sense for any of the others."

"So you all have come to the same conclusion as I have," I pointed out. "I spoke to Forsyth and he admitted to me that he had also arrived at a solution of the case, so I guess he has worked it out as easily as we have."

"So why hasn't MacCallum been arrested and why haven't you presented our solution to the Chief?" complained Beaumont. "It's going to be nice to get our hands on that malt whisky at last."

"As Forsyth pointed out, the case against MacCallum is all circumstantial. The Procurator Fiscal is not going to buy it without a bit more convincing evidence. And I didn't present our solution to the Chief because we can do that at any time before he takes the case to the Chief Super upstairs. I thought that we should spend this evening in trying to make the case watertight. In particular, we should try to have an answer to the things that Forsyth was worried about or indicated were important."

"That seems sensible to me," said Beaumont. "And, if we are going to do that, we need more drink to keep our minds in good nick."

And he went to fetch another round. When he returned and we had all had a drink, I mentioned the first item.

"Why were two panes of glass removed from the French window? Malcolm's theory was that two people were involved and he nominated the Douglases as the culprits. But it is now clear that they were not responsible for the death. So, have we another pair in mind or are we looking for a different explanation of why two panes were cut out?"

There was a pause before anyone spoke and then Jenkins came in.

"I still think that the best explanation is that two people were involved in fishing for the key. MacCallum's wife suffered as much as he did from his losing the tenancy of the hotel. She now is in poor health. She seems the obvious candidate for the role of the second person."

I was a bit sceptical about a frail woman, not in the best of health, being involved in a break-in followed by a murder and torture but, having no better suggestion to offer, kept silent.

As I have said earlier, Fletcher is the least bright of the team but he often comes up with the brightest of ideas. He did so now.

"To get the key," he said rather tentatively, "the killer would have had to poke his head and one arm through the space where the pane had been. For a normal person, this would be no problem. But MacCallum was a big man to start with and, as host of the Merton Arms, drinking with the clientele, would have added quite a lot to his waist line and the upper part of his body. He might find it very difficult to get his head and an arm through the gap in the door and so cut out a second pane so that he could put the head through one and the arm through the other."

"That seems to me," said Beaumont, "to be a much more likely suggestion than that two people were involved. Why would they both need to help in getting the key when one of them could do it on his own quite easily? No I like Sid's idea. It has the ring of truth about it."

I thought as well that Sid's idea made much more sense than that two people had been involved and said so. Jenkins was obviously reluctant to have his brain child dismissed in his way but realised that he had better give in gracefully and accepted that we should go with Sid's explanation.

"With that out of the way," I said, "Anyone got any observations about the knot that the killer used to tie up Merton?"

Jenkins came in like a flash. His explanation of the two panes having bitten the dust, he was keen to show that he was still on the ball and full of brilliant ideas. It was obvious that he had done a bit of research on knots and didn't want to be upstaged by anyone else who had done likewise.

"I had a bit of trawl through knots," he said smugly, "and I reckon that the one used on Merton is a variation on the Schwabisch Hitch used by arborists. Since MaCallum was a keen gardener at one time, maybe he was involved with trees. I don't see any connection with any of the other suspects."

"And, of course," I said thoughtfully, "Forsyth never actually said that the knot was of significance in pointing to the killer. So I suggest that we leave it there unless anyone has any better idea."

There was a general shaking of heads.

"So the final clue that we have to wrestle with

is the book found in Inglis' bedroom after his murder. It was a hardback addition of 'Mary Poppins' by P L Travers and, when I asked Forsyth about it, he said that he believed that Inglis had left the book as a clue for us. Can anyone see how that book points to MacCallum?"

There was a long pause before anyone was prepared to stick his neck out. Not unexpectedly, it was Jenkins who decided to have a go.

"If the book is a clue," he said cautiously, "it would have to be a bit obscure. Otherwise the message it contained would be perfectly obvious to the killer and the book would have been removed when the murderer left the scene."

"That makes good sense to me," I was forced to admit.

"It is most likely that it is the title that holds the clue that Inglis left for us," Jenkins went on. "And a large part of the title of the book is 'poppin'. What is an alternative expression for 'pop in'? It is 'call in' and that sounds just like Colin which is MacCallum's

Christian name."

There was a bit of a silence while we absorbed what Jenkins had said.

"It's a bit convoluted," I said at length. "But, as you pointed out, any message the book contains couldn't be too obvious or the killer would have spotted it and removed the book. And, for all we know, MacCallum, because of his first name, might well have been called Poppins or even Mary at school. Kids make up all sorts of names, often quite cruel, and often quite obscure, for their fellows. It will be Jenkins' task for tomorrow to find out if MacCallum had a nickname at school and, if so, what it was. Has anyone else a comment to make on Malcolm's explanation for the book or even another interpretation of the meaning of the clue?"

No-one else had a different interpretation of what the book was intended to tell us. Neither of the other two were enamoured of Malcolm's solution but admitted that it was certainly a possible explanation and, lacking anything better, should be put to Forsyth in any solution to the case that I made to him.

# CHAPTER 7

It didn't come as any surprise that the dead body of Turner turned up the next day. What did come as a surprise, to me at any rate, was that it turned up in the flat above the grocer's shop. Since neither Forsyth nor I had anticipated that that was where the body would reappear, I had left no policeman guarding the place. Not that that would have done any good in any case. The killer would merely have dumped the body elsewhere.

But dumped is not the right word. That implies that the killer or killers pushed the body into the place and then made off. That was not what had happened at all.

I was notified by Sergeant Anderson that the body of Turner had appeared on the scene and got the normal procedure started. As I was driving Forsyth down to the town, he suddenly came to life.

"An appropriate quotation came to mind," he said, "when you told me that the grocer's body had been found so soon after the killing at the inn. 'God made the wicked grocer for a mystery and a sign, that men would shun the awful shops and go to inns to dine."

He looked across at me.

"I think that is G K Chesterton," I said after a little thought.

"You are pretty good," he observed.

When we got to Auchenbland, we entered the grocer's shop by the front door. Since the building was a crime scene, there was a bored uniform guarding the premises and eager shoppers were being sent elsewhere. After the usual greeting and explanation of what had happened from Beaumont, we went over to the staircase that led up to the private quarters. When we got there, we found that half of part of the bottom of the staircase was cordoned off with police tape and that the same forensic expert whom we had dealt with before, whom I had now discovered was called John Stables, was kneeling on the lower step inside the taped off area beavering away.

"Why have you cordoned off part of the stair?"

I asked.

"I suggest you go and have a look at the body upstairs," Stables replied. "When you come back down, I will be in a much better position to reveal to you what this is all about."

"Fair enough," I said and we mounted the stairs, went along a corridor and entered the bedroom. Turner's naked body was lying on the bed and it had been subjected to the same tortures as had Ralph Merton and Inglis. The covers and a pillow from the bed and a tee shirt that Turner had used instead of pyjamas lay on the floor. Dr Hay was just straightening up from the body as we entered and he came over to join us.

"Same *modus operandi* as before," he told us. "So it's the same murderer and the same agony for the poor bastard on the bed. And same lack of clues for you lot. And, before you ask, the death occurred around 2 am. I will leave you to your work and get on my way. I am, as always, busy. But they do say that a busy man has no time to form bad habits."

Without thinking, I said, "Andre Maurois."

They both stared at me.

"I am impressed," commented Forsyth.

"So they do have the odd educated bloke in the CID," said Hay as he proceeded to get out a cheroot and light it. "Apart from you, of course, Forsyth," he added hastily. "One does keep getting surprised."

And with that he was off leaving the smell of cheap tobacco smoke behind him.

Forsyth had a brief look around. But, since there was nothing that provided any stimulation to his mind, he soon suggested that there was nothing to be gained by staying there and that it would be a good idea to find out what it was that Stables had found downstairs in the shop. So we wended our way down the stairs again. Stables got up from his recumbent position as we neared the foot of the steps.

"It appears," he told us, "that the killer came in by the front door of the shop carrying Turner. So he must have acquired a key to the place from somewhere. Probably Turner had it on him when he was abducted. As he went up the stairs, it seems that the killer stumbled and lost his balance and both of them tumbled down to the foot of the staircase. If you examine the body on the bed upstairs, you will find that it has a number of bruises which were acquired at that time."

"And do you think that the killer suffered any bruising or other injury?" I asked.

"I don't know about bruising but he cut himself in the fall. There are signs that he has cleaned up some blood that was spilt on the last step and the floor. He has done it so well that I doubt that I will even be able to tell you what his blood group is."

"But if our killer was bleeding that badly, he would need to put something over the wound to stop the flow," suggested the Chief. "Have you any idea what he would have used?"

Stables motioned us to follow him and went over to where a First Aid box was hanging on the wall. It stood open and we saw that it was not as comprehensively filled with pharmalogical goodies as a safety officer would have liked. Forsyth took out each item that the box contained and examined it before putting it back.

What the box contained was a bottle of iodine, a paper container that held a large amount of cotton wool, a packet of aspirin and one of cocodamol, a pair of scissors on which the blades appeared to be very loose, a couple of cotton bandages and a card of safety pins.

"It also held another smaller bandage," Stables informed us, "and a roll of adhesive tape, according to Esther Murray who found the body when she came in to work as usual this morning. By the way, she was very upset at finding the body of her employer in such a state and seemed on the verge of hysterics, so I thought it prudent to send her home."

"That was the sensible thing to have done," said Forsyth.

"And your thinking," I guessed, "is that the killer had used that missing bandage to cover the bleeding wound and then held it in place by sticking it down with the adhesive tape."

Stables motioned to us again to follow him and led us to one of the counters. On it lay a large knife, that had obviously been used for some interesting purpose by the grocer and by the killer to cut a portion from the roll of adhesive tape that lay beside it. It was clear that the knife was not the sharpest I had ever seen because the end of the tape was by no means a straight line and showed a number of places where random pieces of all shapes and sizes had been removed from it. There were several cuts visible on the surface of the counter.

"As you can see, he just chopped off the size of piece that he needed."

"And didn't leave a solitary fingerprint for us," I guessed.

"Not a sausage. He wore gloves, I reckon, like most villains these days."

The Chief mooned around the shop after looking carefully at the tape on the counter. When he was satisfied that he had seen all there was to see, we left and went to interview a tearful Esther Murray at her house. But, although she gave, through a continual outburst of sobs, an account of finding the body, she had no information that was of any interest to us. So we went back to the car to return to Edinburgh. Once we were well on our way, I asked Forsyth whether the latest murder had yielded anything that would lead him to be prepared to present his case to the Procurator Fiscal.

"I am now of the opinion," he said carefully, "the latest killing having given me a further piece of evidence, that I can present a case to the Procurator Fiscal which will be good enough for him to decide to prosecute."

I was unable to bring to mind anything that I had seen that day that would constitute good enough new evidence to gladden the heart of a Procurator Fiscal to such an extent that he would be prepared to take the case to court.

"If you have got to that stage," I said hurriedly, "perhaps you would be prepared to listen to a solution to the case that has been arrived at by your team after considerable discussion."

"I would be delighted to listen to any solution you come up with. It will pass the time most agreeably on our journey to Headquarters. In addition, as you are well aware, I always find it fascinating to see how that mind of yours works."

He settled comfortably back in his seat, closed his eyes and brought the fingertips of his two hands together in his lap. I took a deep breath, collected my thoughts and tried to put forward our case in the most interesting and rational way that I could. He appeared to be listening intently. When I had finished, he lay without moving for a few minutes and then opened his eyes and straightened up in his seat.

"Your theory is ingenious, as always. I find it pleasing that you are using your mind and not letting it ossify through neglect."

"And I gather from that that you do not agree with our conclusions and that you have arrived at a quite different solution."

"That is so."

"So where did we go wrong?"

"Firstly, I find your reason why two panes of glass were removed from the French window unconvincing. All that is required for the operation of getting the key is that the intruder should be able to get his implement for fishing for the key, followed by his arm and his head, through the gap made by the removal of the pane. MacCallum was a large man but where he had expanded most was in the region of his belly. The upper part of his body was not so large that he could not get his head and one arm through the gap, possibly with a slight squeeze."

"But that is not your only objection. I gather from your use of the word 'firstly'."

"Since MacCallum had a right to feel a grievance against the two Mertons and, to a lesser extent, Inglis because of the way in which he had been treated, one can understand why he would torture and then kill them," Forsyth pointed out. "But why would he do the same to Turner with whom he had no quarrel? Why did he not just kill him wherever it was that they came across each other? And, in particular, why would he take him back to his own house to conduct the torture and murder when that markedly increased the possibility of him and his captive being spotted and the police being informed?"

While he was giving this criticism of our theory, an interesting new idea had occurred to me. I was doing some fast thinking, trying to add a bit more flesh to the skeleton that I had come up with.

"Maybe McCallum and Mathers were in it together," I came in quickly. "In that case, Mathers would want his revenge on Turner, who had taken away his livelihood, as much as MacCallum wanted revenge on Inglis. And the two panes of glass were removed from the French window so that the two could take part together in the getting of the key."

"I should have thought," retorted Forsyth, "that one person could fish the key from its hook more easily than two acting together. With two involved, their actions would need to be coordinated and, without perfect timing, each one would be likely to get in the other's way.

"I am also not totally convinced that, although MacCallum and Mathers might feel enough hatred for the Mertons to wish to torture and kill them, they would feel the part played by Inglis and Turner was sufficient to merit the same punishment. Murder, perhaps, for their part in doing him down but why the torture?"

"You may well have a point there," I was prepared to concede.

"And, finally, your explanation of the clue that the book contained, namely that Poppins was supposed to suggest Colin, verges on the puerile."

"So we got nothing right."

"A good effort nonetheless and ingenious. And

I always like to see my team attempting to beat me to a solution."

"It does look," I said ruefully, "as if your malt whisky can stay safely in your cellar. When are you going to reveal all?"

"I shall be buying drinks in the usual hostelry at 5.30 this evening. If it would interest you, I will reveal my solution to you all at that time."

I was particularly taken by the 'If it would interest you'. That really was rich. The purpose of the meeting was not only so that he could reward the team for work well done but much more so that he could impress us with the magnificence of his reasoning. If he had to tie us down to keep us there, he would ensure that we were not released until we had heard his solution and marvelled at his brilliance.

Nothing necessary to the solution of the reason for the murders and the arson attack has been withheld in the previous chapters. It is therefore possible for the reader to arrive by logical deduction at the name of the murderer and an explanation of all the known facts. If you decide try to do so, good luck.

# CHAPTER 8

At 5.30 that evening the team were seated round the table that we always chose in our usual watering hole, pints of heavy in front of three of us and a gin and tonic in front of the fourth. On the table, by the empty place that we had left, sat a large glass of Glenlivet malt whisky, Forsyth's favourite. The Chief buying us a drink is not quite as simple as it might seem. True, he will eventually buy a round, two if the meeting is prolonged. But he expects that a drink will be waiting for him when he arrives.

The great man eventually appeared in the doorway and looked around. Since he knows perfectly well the table we always occupy, the pause at the entrance is to allow the other denizens of the pub to have time to see which personality it was who had decided to grace them with his presence. Since he had not yet appeared on television in connection with the current case and it was some time since he had been seen on the box, and the frequenters of bars have short memories, no interest was shown in the new arrival. Forsyth accepted philosophically that he was not going to enjoy a triumphal entry and strolled over to our table.

Having greeted us warmly, he sat down and took a substantial swallow from the malt whisky. He put the glass down, smiled at us and spoke.

"I have just come from explaining my solution of the case to the Chief Constable and the Chief Superintendent, a task that is not the easiest in the world since neither is endowed with a brain that finds it easy to follow logical argument. But irrespective of how much they really understood of my reasoning, they are naturally delighted that a difficult case has been brought to a successful conclusion and they wished their congratulations for the good work that the team has done should be conveyed to you by me at this time."

"We didn't do much," I pointed out ruefully.

"Your contribution was, as usual, invaluable. They also serve who only stand and wait."

"Milton," was my automatic response, but I

said it under my breath.

"But you are, no doubt, eager to hear who was responsible for these murders and how I succeeded in arriving at his name."

No doubt to increase the tension that he supposed we were feeling, he paused for a few moments in order to imbibe another substantial quantity of malt whisky before continuing.

"There were two matters that seemed to me of interest after the first murder that we had to investigate. The first was why two panes of glass, and not just one, had been removed from the French window in order to gain entry to the Merton house. One recalls that, standing outside the window, the key that would open the door was situated on a hook to the left of the window on the inner side of the outside wall. It struck me that, while it would be easy for a right-handed person to put his head and right arm through the gap and pick from its hook the desired key, it would be very much more difficult for a left-handed person to do so because the left arm bends in the wrong way for such an exercise. So that a left-handed person might well cut out two panes of glass so that he could put the left arm through one and the right through the other and use both hands to hold the pole or wire that was used to fish for the key."

"It makes sense," said Jenkins, "but it is something that I didn't think of."

"That, of course, is the difference between us," said Forsyth rather rudely. "If you wish to succeed in this game, you must think of all possibilities. The second thing that was of interest was the unusual knot found on the rope used to tie up Ralph Merton. That seemed to imply that the murderer was someone who, in his public or private life, was involved in an activity that needed him to familiarise himself with the tying of knots. You can therefore imagine my pleasure in finding that one of our suspects was not only left-handed but was also a keen fly fisherman and many of that breed tie their own flies."

"You are talking of Goff," I exclaimed. "He batted left-handed for the cricket team and had been president of the local angling club."

"Precisely. But, before I proceed, I note that your glasses are almost empty. Perhaps, Mr Fletcher, you would be good enough to go to the bar and purchase large malt whiskies for everyone unless Mr Jenkins would prefer a further gin and tonic."

Jenkins indicated that he would. It was clear that the Chief found it difficult to believe that any Scotsman would make that choice, but made no overt remark He handed over some banknotes and Fletcher went off to the bar. It was only after he had returned and distributed the drinks all round that Forsyth resumed his narrative.

"As I explained to Sergeant MacRae at the time, and he has no doubt explained to you since, the fire was not intended to wipe out the rest of the Merton family but was merely done to make us believe that the Douglases were to blame for it, and therefore, by extension, for the previous two murders and to divert us from any suspicion we might have for the real reason for the killings."

He paused and had another drink of malt whisky before resuming.

"I have to admit that I had not envisaged the death of Inglis and was rather taken aback when it occurred. I even for a moment questioned whether I had been somehow misled after the first murder. But my reasoning there seemed to be correct  But, even although reporting a crime for which you were sent to prison didn't seem to me to be  a very good motive for killing the two people involved, I could imagine that an unbalanced person might well see it differently.  But I could initially see no reason why Goff should then go on to murder Inglis with whom he seemed to have no quarrel "

"And something that I said appeared to resolve the difficulty for you," I came in.

"You mentioned coincidence and I reflected that it had seemed to me something of a coincidence that at roughly the same time that Goff was involved in a traffic accident in which a child was killed, the Mertons should choose that time to throw people out of occupations that they had held for some years and in which at least some of those involved had been doing quite well."

"And did you come to the conclusion that it wasn't just a coincidence?" enquired Beaumont.

"I did," Forsyth told him. "As I said earlier, I found it difficult to believe that Goff, or anyone else for that matter, would feel so vindictive towards the pair who had shopped him that he would not only kill them but very brutally torture them as well. But it made good sense if Goff was telling the truth that he had never killed the child. What if one of the Mertons, probably Ethan since he was the one who drove around at high speed, had knocked down the child and then, along with his brother, had framed Goff for the crime."

"I don't see how that explains him killing Inglis," said a rather befogged Fletcher.

"It makes sense if you assume that there were witnesses to the accident in which Ethan Merton was involved. If Inglis and Turner, who were friends, were out together and saw the accident happen, they would have to agree to the framing of Goff and would have to be bought off by offering them, probably in addition to a fair amount of money, the opportunity to run businesses in Auchenbland.  This would entail the removal of the current holders of the tenancies and it would be necessary to throw others out of jobs and houses as well in order to obscure what you were doing and why you were doing it.  And if, at some later time, Goff got to know that witnesses had allowed themselves to be bribed and had not spoken up in his defence, he would have as great a hatred against them as he had against the Mertons."

"Weren't you making a hell a lot of assumptions without all that much evidence," I suggested, "in order to justify your picking on Goff as the killer after the first murder, a piece of reasoning that might have been quite wrong?"

He bridled.

"My reasoning is never wrong," he insisted. He was beginning to believe the myth that he had so carefully created.

"And I never choose my facts," he went on, "in such a way as to justify anything. But, since I knew at that time that Goff was definitely the man we were looking for, I had to find sensible reasons for the savagery of his revenge and the reason why he would also extend that revenge to Inglis and Turner."

"How could you possibly know that Goff was our man?" demanded Jenkins.

"Because of the clue to his killer that Inglis left in the form of a book."

"How on earth does Mary Poppins tell you that Goff is the murderer?"

"The author of Mary Poppins was a very determined lady who had a running battle with Walt Disney over his attempts to persuade her to allow him to make a film of the book. But P L Travers was merely a pen name that she used. Her real name was Helen Goff."

"Of course it was," said Jenkins. Whether he had really known this I took leave to doubt.

"I was also confirmed in my view that my solution was the correct one," Forsyth carried on, "by the disappearance of Mr Turner."

"So you don't believe," I suggested, "that Turner was out and about that night and saw Goff in or near Inglis' house?"

"I do not. Turner no doubt believed that the murders of the Mertons were the work of the Douglases or some disgruntled person like Grant. But, if he had been left at large after Inglis had been killed, the penny would have dropped and Turner would have come running to us with the name of Goff on his lips."

"So he had to get Turner out of the way that very evening."

"He broke into the grocer's shop through an unlocked window and removed him to a hiding place that he had earlier prepared. He probably hadn't the time, nor the stomach," Forsyth argued, "to deal with Turner after he had tortured Inglis. And he was very keen to give the impression that the killing of Turner was not part of his original plan but had been forced on him by events. If we believed that, it made it less likely that we would see the whole picture and realise that Goff was the man behind all the killings."

"But at that stage you believed," I reminded him, "that the case was not such that the Procurator Fiscal was likely to take it up and prosecute. What did you glean from the final murder that persuaded you otherwise?"

"During the course of organising the final murder, Goff slipped and fell while carrying Turner upstairs from the shop to the bedroom. As a result of the fall, he suffered a wound which bled and which had to be covered up by a bandage held in place by tape. The piece of tape that Goff required had to be cut from a roll and Goff did this with considerable difficulty by slicing off on the counter the bit he required using a rather blunt knife. The end left was ragged and showed that Goff had had a lot of bother in cutting the piece that he wanted. So why did he not use the scissors that were in the same First Aid box in which he had found the bandage and the tape?"

He paused dramatically and waited for a response to his question from one of the team. When none came, he smiled triumphantly and continued.

"Many left-handed people find it difficult, if not impossible, to use the normal right-handed scissors, particularly if the blades are rather loosely joined. They have to use specially made left-handed scissors. Goff is clearly one of these persons. The fact that he used a blunt knife, not the best of things to use to cut tape, when a pair of scissors was available and in full view, is a clear indication that the killer was left-handed. And that is a demonstration that a jury can follow and understand easily."

"So presumably Goff has been arrested," said Beaumont.

"I got the local police to bring him in. When I presented my case to him, he did not attempt to argue the toss and deny it. He confessed that he had been responsible for the deaths and insisted that all the victims had deserved everything that he had done to them for framing him for a crime that he had not committed and causing enormous distress, not only to him, but to the rest of his family."

"Did he explain how he had come to carry out the murder of Ethan Merton," I asked.

"He told me that for some time he had been thinking of exacting revenge on the people who had framed him but had lacked the impulse that would have got him started. Then, on the night that Ethan had had that final row with his family, Goff was out late after doing a 'homer' on the car of an acquaintance. Ethan, driving away from the estate in a wild fury had almost run him down and had stopped to see that he was all right. Goff was a bit shaken but otherwise  fine. But, when Ethan said that  he was going to Edinburgh Airport  to see about flying to South America, Goff saw his opportunity and asked if he could get a lift to the capital. Ethan obvously felt that he shoild be generous to someone he had alsost run over. And, of course, he had no idea that Goff had found out how he had been set up.

"When they got near the airport, Goff persuaded him to stop, overpowered him, tortured him and then killed him. Corstorphine Hill was the nearest piece of open ground, so he buried him there, left the car in the garage at the airport and got the first bus home."

There was a silence while we all marvelled at the ease with which Forsyth had solved the crime that had sent the rest of us up a blind alley.

"So this has been another triumph to be added to the long list of your successes," I eventually said admiringly.

He tried to look modest but without achieving much success.

It was at that moment that a couple of men I

had never seen before entered the bar, one carrying a camera and, after looking around, came over to our table. They introduced themselves as Bill Jefferson and Martin Bates and explained that they were from the news section of BBC Scotland. Forsyth welcomed them to the table.

"They said that they wanted to interview me about the fact that we had managed to solve the latest case," Forsyth explained to us. "I suggested that the best place to conduct the interview would be here with the rest of the team present so that you could answer any additional questions that might arise concerning matters that one or other of you had investigated. If Mr Jefferson will buy us drinks all round so that we are in a suitable mood to be interviewed, I think that we can get started. I will have a large Glenlivet. What would the rest of you like?"

We made our wishes known, Jefferson produced some money and Fletcher went off to fetch the drinks. I settled back to enjoy the next half hour.

And I had to hand it to Forsyth.  He had made sure that, although he would be paid nothing for the interview, all of us would gain a little happiness from the event.